THE FARMING MURDER

A gripping crime mystery full of twists

(Eric Ward Book 2)

ROY LEWIS

Revised edition 2019
Joffe Books, London
www.joffebooks.com

First published as "Dwell in Danger" 1982

We hate typos too but sometimes they slip through.
Please send any errors you find to
corrections@joffebooks.com
We'll get them fixed ASAP. We're very grateful to
eagle-eyed readers who take the time to contact us.

**Please join our mailing list for free Kindle crime thriller,
detective, and mystery books and new releases.**
http://www.joffebooks.com/contact/

ISBN: 978-1-78931-144-0

NOTE TO THE READER

Please note this book is set in the early 1980s in England, a time before mobile phones and DNA testing, and when social attitudes were very different.

Affection dwells in danger

Thomas Carlyle

CHAPTER 1

It was not an easy decision to take.

Advising other people what they should do was a large part of Eric Ward's life: they came to him in his office, laid bare the most intimate details of their married lives, disclosed criminal offences, told him about the business contracts they had foolishly entered into, insisted they had not read the terms of the hire purchase contract on which they were being sued, denied that they had allowed the drains to become blocked and overflow on to the neighbouring property. He gave them the advice they sought, soothed them, calmed them, explained the law to them and, when they insisted, agreed to act for them in the ensuing litigation.

None of that was a problem. He was good at taking decisions for other people. But it was a different matter when he was the subject of the problem.

The sun was warm on the back of his head as he walked along the Quayside. He had parked near Dog Leap Stairs, unwilling to go back immediately to the office after his appointment with Mr Callaghan. The river sparkled in the sunshine; a freighter lay moored near the High Level Bridge, and up above the cars and lorries thundered and roared across the river, speeding past the old law courts, scene of countless assizes, past the church where the Lord High Chancellor of England had married his sweetheart, past the bank where sixteenth-century cottages still huddled precariously together under the steep slopes below the Moot Hall.

He looked up and the sky above was an intense, aching blue; the vapour trail of a jet etched its track, slowly stitching its way across the vast distances. The sharp blue made his eyes hurt and he felt the prickle of involuntary tears.

No, it was not an easy decision to take, when your pride and your life and your future lay at stake.

Callaghan had been fair, and honest — as professional as Eric himself was, in his own professional circumstances. But it made it no easier a decision — though at least Eric had all the facts at his disposal. He smiled ruefully, turning to pace back towards his car. A lawyer was supposed to have a trained, logical mind, capable of evaluating facts and reaching decisions.

He had the facts.

* * *

Philippa was small, plump, pretty and flustered. She had been with Francis, Shaw and Elder for almost two years now, joining just when Eric Ward had qualified as a solicitor, and though she did a competent, workmanlike job as a legal executive-cum-personal secretary, there was still an underlying nervousness in her which surfaced whenever things were not going right.

She was fluttering outside Eric's office as he made his way up the stairs. He smiled at her, encouragingly. 'They're not due yet, are they, Philippa?'

'No, Mr Ward. Another forty minutes. But ... I've put all I can find on your desk. I hope—'

'It will be all right, I'm certain,' Eric reassured her, and made his way into his room.

He walked to the window and stood looking out for a few minutes, still unwilling to let Callaghan's words drift away from him, still wanting to see a swift, determined solution to the problem, but knowing at the same time there was none. Then, shaking his head he turned, sat down behind his desk and reached for the manila folders that Philippa had left on his desk.

An index; a sheaf of papers; references. Patiently, Eric began to read through the papers, skimming swiftly over the cogent details, familiarizing himself with the legal history, as known to Francis, Shaw and Elder, of the Saxby family, of Morpeth.

The papers ended in 1946.

Frowning, Eric checked the file index again. Then he leaned back in his chair, thinking. After a few minutes he pressed the intercom button; there was a short delay and then the rasping, slightly impatient voice came over to him.

'Yes?'

'Joseph — could you spare me a few minutes?'

'Right now?'

'I'd appreciate it. I have a client coming in to see me in about thirty minutes, and I'd like to have a word with you first.'

'Humph ... You'd better come straight up, then.'

Eric went straight up.

Joseph Francis was not busy. As the senior partner in Francis, Shaw and Elder he clearly believed he had spent his years in the front line and had earned his medals: now, he kept just a few of the trust files, and undertook some of the commercial work — that work which involved largely PR activity. His narrow, patrician face was often photographed in the company of important businessmen in Newcastle; his neatly parted, silvery hair regularly shone from the pages of *Newcastle Life*, at Heart Foundation dances, Chamber of Commerce meetings, Masonic activities. There were some in the rapidly expanding firm who believed he was now past it, legally: Eric Ward was not among them. Joseph Francis had slowed down, certainly, but he still possessed a keen legal brain and if he affected a smoothly modulated voice, a slightly bored air, Eric at least was not fooled by it. Joseph Francis used his junior partners to make money for him, but he could still do it himself, if he wanted, or needed to.

The senior partner waved Eric to a chair. 'What's the problem?'

'I've got someone called Saxby coming to see me shortly.' Eric said.

'Amos Saxby?'

'No. Jack Saxby.'

'One of his sons. Well?'

'The Saxby files seem to be somewhat thin.'

Joseph Francis frowned, allowing his normally unruffled features to express a hint of concern. 'What's Jack Saxby coming to see you about?'

'I don't know. That's why I asked Philippa to dig out the back files. I've had no dealings with the Saxbys previously and I couldn't find much, so—'

'She checked upstairs in the old files?' Joseph Francis interrupted and for a moment something flickered in his eyes as he recalled an occasion when he had quarrelled with Eric Ward over the matter of Egan administration. He sniffed. 'Nothing up there?'

Eric shrugged. 'I asked Philippa to check. She produced some files, but they seem to end in 1946.'

'Saxby,' Joseph Francis mused. He stared at his immaculate fingernails thoughtfully. 'I did some work for Amos Saxby years ago ... for that matter, there was his father too, when I was just a young, newly-fledged solicitor myself. The Saxbys have been with us a while, you might say.'

'I gather there was some kind of trust fund.'

'That's right.' Joseph Francis leaned back in his chair, steepled his fingers under his chin. 'Over the years, there's been a bit of money in that family. The grandfather was a brewer, in the Midlands; he married a farmer's daughter from Staffordshire or somewhere and when he retired he came to live with his son, who had taken to farming, in Northumberland. There was a trust fund established — not

4

terribly well managed, I might add, so the old man finally came to us after certain problems arose and we sacked the trustees, took over ourselves. When the old man died, a couple of farms came to Amos Saxby — but what he's done with them I can't imagine, for he must be near retirement age now. Though you can't tell with some of these farmers, can you?'

Or lawyers, his cool eyes suddenly seemed to challenge.

Eric ignored the challenge. 'The files end in 1946. But according to the index, we've certainly acted for the Saxbys since then. As recently as two, three years ago, as far as I can make out.'

'And the files aren't there?'

'They might have been misfiled; mislaid; or maybe they've been extracted.'

'But a note should have been made in that case,' Joseph snapped, a hint of anger staining his voice. 'What was the last annotation?'

Eric hesitated. 'It ... it looks like Paul's handwriting.'

Again there was a movement in Joseph Francis's old eyes, but it was swiftly suppressed. It was two years now since Paul Francis had left his father's firm. It had always been a problem for Joseph wanting to see Paul come in, qualified, to take over the reins when Joseph himself had retired, and then to come to the slow realization that Paul was simply not cut out to be a solicitor. He had qualified all right, but he had lacked the *application* to make a success of the job. Eric Ward had come into the firm with a degree won by part-time study after a career in the police force and Paul Francis had immediately felt inferior. It had been reflected in his attitudes towards Eric, and the manner in which he avoided the basic but essential drudgery of much of the work, passing it to Eric.

Shortly before Eric had finally qualified, Paul had announced his intention to go to the Bar, where his personality and talents might be better employed. Joseph had financed him, and Paul was now in practice. It was early days, but he seemed to be making a reasonable fist of it in local chambers, with the assistance of the odd brief from Francis, Shaw and Elder. Joseph Francis believed in looking after his own.

It was why he now avoided Eric's eye. 'Well, I've no doubt the missing files will turn up. I'll give Paul a ring this evening, see if he remembers. Might even go around for a chat. There'll be an explanation ... but meanwhile, do you *need* the damned files?'

'I don't know. Philippa didn't get from John Saxby the reason for the visit.'

'Well, then, dammit,' Joseph Francis said sharply, 'there's not much point in this conversation, is there?'

'I merely thought—'

But Joseph Francis's cold eyes cut him short. You merely thought, they said, that you would bring to my attention as senior partner the suggestion of incompetence on the part of my son. Eric rose, shrugging slightly, and turned to leave the room.

'You'll let me know,' Joseph said, 'if the visit does have anything to do with the missing files? I'll check with Paul in any case.'

'I'll let you know.'

Eric had reached the door when Joseph called his name again. He turned, and Joseph was rising, moving towards the window. 'Eric ...' He seemed vaguely uncomfortable. 'You ... you were out of the office this morning.'

'That's right.'

'I ... er ... I don't wish to give the impression that I was prying, but I wanted a word with you on the Cartwright Trust and they told me at reception that you'd gone out, to Gosforth. They said you'd gone to see a Mr Callaghan, in Elm Tree House.'

Eric stared woodenly at the senior partner, and nodded. 'That's right.'

Joseph Francis moistened his lips with a pink tongue. 'I know a Mr Callaghan ... Masonic connections ... He's an eye specialist.'

Eric nodded, but made no reply.

'Things are ... no better?' Joseph Francis ventured. 'I mean—'

'There are problems,' Eric said curtly. There had been problems ever since that day when George Knox, the police surgeon, had first diagnosed glaucoma and told Eric that his career in the police force was over. There had been the problem of finding a new job, carving out a new life for himself at the age of forty. There had been the long hours sweating over his external law degree, suffering from the physical pressures that evening study presented. There had been the blinding headaches, the pain scratching at the back of his eyes like cat's claws, unsheathed and tearing, and the nausea and vomiting in the hours of darkness when his spirits were at their lowest ebb and despair reached out and took him by the throat. He had stared in the mirror and disbelieved the evidence of the red, swollen eyelids, the greenish discolouration of the iris, the hardness of the eyeballs, but in some ways the worst thing of all had been the blow to his pride and his manhood. Six feet tall, with a lean, hard-muscled body and a knowledge of his own physical fitness during his years on the force — and then to face the unacceptable fact that he was destined to go blind. Yes, there had been problems, and they were not over.

'What did Mr Callaghan ... er ... what did he tell you, Eric?' Joseph Francis asked.

He had a right to know. It was his firm. He had taken a chance, offering Eric a partnership when Paul Francis had left the firm, even though Eric knew the offer had been a deserved one. Now, Joseph had a right to know. Eric shrugged, suddenly tired.

'He went over it all again. Just as we lawyers enjoy the legal terminology, so surgeons too, they like to explain in detail. So I got the causes of glaucoma again: local congestion blocking the canal of Schlemm as the iris is pushed forward; the cornea unable to allow escape of fluids; the pressure building up, eating away at the optic nerves. I've heard it before: a classical case of chronic glaucoma.'

'And?'

'We discussed treatment again ... my use of pilocarpine, to relieve the pressure. He carried out some tests on me, questioned me pretty closely. And then we talked about iridectomy.'

'My medical knowledge ...' Joseph Francis murmured, after a short silence.

'It's the treatment for acute glaucoma,' Eric explained. 'It involves the removal of a small section of the iris. That allows the fluid to escape. And in the case of chronic glaucoma they'd have to use a filtration procedure as well, to establish a new drainage path for the fluid. And as you know,' Eric added, 'that's what I've got. Chronic glaucoma.'

'What er — what does Mr Callaghan now recommend?' Joseph Francis asked.

Eric managed a faint smile. 'That's the problem. He's not prepared to recommend anything. As he puts it, the results of surgery in a case like mine are less than certain.'

'So if you have the operation?'

'I could go blind.'

'And if you do not?'

Eric shrugged. 'The physical position is deteriorating. He wouldn't set a time scale to it but he's pretty positive it's going to happen, and sooner rather than later. But ... he won't take the responsibility of advising. He's given me all the facts.'

'And the decision,' Joseph Francis said softly, 'is yours.'

'That puts it,' Eric Ward said, 'in the traditional nutshell.'

* * *

The investigation that morning had placed a strain on Eric Ward; the discussion thereafter, the need to face up to a decision was causing him further stress. There was still a short time left before Jack Saxby came to see him and there were intimations that Eric might have an attack again soon: the pain was not reaching out to him yet but the prickling was there at his nerve ends, the long-accepted prelude to the exquisite darts of agony that would shear through his eyes in a little while. He opened his desk drawer and took out the bottle of pilocarpine, inserted the end of the eye-dropper and brought up a quantity of the drug.

The fluid dripped into the corner of his eyes; he began to tremble, the natural reaction to the tension that always gripped him at the onset of pain. He had never overcome the reaction, based as it was upon hysteria. It was something again that gnawed at his pride.

In a little while the prickling had ended. The intercom buzzed, and Philippa announced the arrival of Mr and Mrs Saxby.

Jack Saxby wore his blue suit uneasily. It was the uniform he had donned to visit a solicitor, his compliance with form, but he would clearly have been much more at home in an open-necked shirt and sweater, corduroy trousers and wellington boots. He was shorter than Eric Ward by perhaps five inches but his upper body was broad and powerfully muscled, straining at the shoulders of the suit. The collar of his shirt was tight at his thick neck and his pale blue eyes were nervous, but there was a dogged honesty of purpose in those eyes too, that Eric liked. Jack Saxby came forward and offered his hand: thick-fingered, firm in its grasp, it matched the general image Jack Saxby presented. He was a no-nonsense Northumbrian, clear-eyed and fair-minded; a skin tanned and lined by wind and sun on the high hills demonstrated his background, the jut of his jaw emphasized his determination.

'This is my wife, Sandra.'

She did not look like a farmer's wife. She was slight, as tall as her husband, but her skin was fair, her frame almost willowy. She wore her hair long, scraped back into a black ponytail that belied her age — for she and her husband, Eric calculated, were in their mid-thirties. She also lacked the directness of her husband in some uncertain manner: perhaps it was the way she did not meet Eric's glance other than briefly; perhaps it was the feeling of tension he detected, induced possibly by the office in which she found herself.

But there was something else too: the line of her mouth expressed a dissatisfaction that Eric considered was probably deep-seated. Its origins would lie beyond the reason for their visit this day to Francis, Shaw and Elder.

Eric asked them to sit down and then buzzed Philippa, asking her to bring in some coffee.

'I'd prefer tea, if you don't mind,' Jack Saxby said hesitantly.

Eric glanced towards Sandra Saxby but she shook her head. She did not look at her husband but her back was stiff.

'Make it two coffees, Philippa,' Eric said, 'and one tea.' He switched off the intercom and smiled at Jack Saxby. He gestured towards the files on his desk. 'I've brought in the papers dealing with previous Saxby transactions handled by us, but I'm afraid I don't know whether they're relevant. You didn't tell my secretary the purpose of your call today, so—'

'That's right.' Jack Saxby frowned. 'Have you handled any of my father's business before?'

Eric shook his head. 'No. Saxby affairs were dealt with by another partner. I'm new to it all, so you'll have to bear with me—'

'That's no matter,' Jack Saxby interrupted. 'All to the good, really.'

Eric waited and a little silence fell. A fly buzzed against the window, seeking the sunshine. 'So how can I help you, Mr Saxby?' Eric asked.

'You don't know no background about us?'

'If you can fill whatever necessary—'

'You'll know my father Amos was a farmer, up Morpeth way. Retired two years ago,' Jack Saxby said, frowning. 'He's about sixty-eight now, old warhorse, tough as old boots. My mother—'

'That would be—'

'Ellen Saxby. She's maybe ten years younger than the old man. They was farming together for years, but retired to a house in Morpeth; no money problems, investments, rents, that sort of thing. But that's by the way.' Jack Saxby fixed Eric with a sudden, intense glare. 'I want some advice, Mr Ward. Fact is, I think I'm being done down!' He shot a glance at his wife and then repeated, 'Done down.'

The door opened and Philippa walked in. Eric waited until his clients had been served with their respective cups and then sipped his own coffee. As the door closed again he asked, 'Just exactly what do you mean, Mr Saxby?'

'It's the old man,' Sandra Saxby said, thin-lipped. 'It's his doing.'

'Things aren't so simple—'

Sandra Saxby cut across her husband's reluctant remonstration. 'He talked her into it, I know it.'

Eric was aware of the tension rising between husband and wife and he pushed his coffee aside. 'Perhaps you'd better tell me the whole story.'

Jack Saxby glanced uncertainly at his wife and then nodded.

'It goes back a few years, you understand. My father, Amos, he was left a fair bit of land — couple of farms which he worked most of his life. My mother, she didn't have much at all, not until about fifteen years or so ago. She had a cousin, you see—'

'He was called Frank Jennings,' Sandra Saxby said. 'He was an estate agent at Corbridge for most of his life, but took to farming late on, and made a good job of it.'

Jack Saxby nodded. 'He did that. And he died—'

'In 1967,' Sandra affirmed, at her husband's hesitation.

'That's right. 1967. Anyway,' Jack Saxby continued, 'there was a will and I think it was your firm that did all the necessary legal things to sort it out. Upshot was that he left this farm—'

'Holton Hill Farm.'

'—Holton Hill Farm to my mother. That meant she was holding land apart from Amos, doesn't it?'

'That's right,' Eric agreed. 'If it was left to her by name she would hold it independently of her husband.'

'Right.' Jack Saxby sipped his tea. 'She put a manager in for a while but it didn't work out too well and I think she had it

11

in mind to sell at one time. Anyway, by then I was married and keen to set up in my own right — I was nineteen and thought I knew it all, so I went and spoke to my mother, and she had words with Amos, and, well, the upshot of it all was that my mother agreed to make over the farm to me as a tenant.'

'You took a lease of Holton Hill Farm from her?'

'That's right—'

'The old man thought Jack couldn't do the job,' Sandra Saxby interposed, 'so it was just a short lease.'

'Three years,' Jack Saxby said. 'Time to give me chance to find my feet, settle down, show I could run the farm. I was only nineteen.'

Sandra Saxby muttered something under her breath. Eric looked at her: she was a good-looking woman, apart from that disconsolate mouth.

'And the problem?' Eric prompted.

Jack Saxby's eyes glistened angrily. 'When the three-year tenancy was up I went to see my mother. She agreed that the farm was run well; Amos agreed that too. So she gave me a new lease. Everything went well after that, and I built up the stock, got a good business going. Then about eight years ago, my mother, she was talking to me, speaking of her and my father retiring, and wanting to make sure that I was properly provided for. So after that she asked me if I'd like to buy Holton Hill Farm from her. I said I couldn't afford it, but she just laughed. Next thing I know is she'd been to your firm and had this drawn up. I got a copy of it.'

He delved in his pocket and extracted a sheet of paper. He handed it across the desk to Eric Ward.

To Jack Saxby, Holton Hill Farm.

In consideration of the sum of one pound paid by you to me I hereby give you the option of purchasing the Holton Hill Farm now in your occupation at the sum of ten pounds (£10) per acre. This option to remain effective for ten years.

Dated this thirteenth day of March, 1974.

Ellen Saxby.

'You can see it signed proper, over a stamp,' Jack Saxby said.

'Yes, it would appear to be in order,' Eric agreed. 'Er ... what is the acreage of Holton Hill Farm?'

'About three hundred acres.'

'What would you calculate its value to be now?'

Jack Saxby hesitated and Sandra Saxby gritted her teeth audibly. 'We reckon about £40,000,' she said.

Eric looked at Jack Saxby. 'Your mother was behaving generously towards you.'

'The story isn't over yet,' Sandra Saxby said bitterly.

Jack Saxby waved his hand to her, irritated, then went on. 'It'll be about five, six years since, I went to see my mother. I told her I'd like to exercise the option that she'd given me. I was prepared to buy the farm from her. She said she'd ask my father. We had a long chat then. He said it wasn't time to go ahead with it then. The thing was, he'd taken advice, and the option thing, it was really only a sort of device, a way of beating death duties. I spoke to my mother and she said, yes, that was part of it, but if I'd be patient she'd let me exercise the option in a little while. I spoke again to them two years later. The old man was still against me buying: he said she ought to treat it as an agricultural investment so as to save death duties.'

Eric nodded. 'Er ... how were relationships between you and your parents at this time? I mean, was there a quarrel?'

Saxby shook his head. 'No, it wasn't like that. They were just ... discussions. I mean, it didn't make much difference. I had the tenancy, I was running the farm, so it didn't matter too much, did it? I had the option, so the farm would come to me in the end.'

'You should have forced them to sell,' Sandra muttered fiercely. 'I told you at the time, but you wouldn't listen. Stick in the bloody mud—'

Hastily Eric said, 'So what happened after that?'

Jack Saxby looked down at his feet. He shook his head. 'I'm not certain. Something happened. There was a row up at Morpeth and the next time I asked my mother about the option she said she didn't want to discuss it. And then ...'

Eric waited; Sandra Saxby stared at her husband but he appeared not to be aware of her presence any longer. His eyes were clouded with memory as he searched back over the past for reasons, explanations, solutions, but the twist in his mouth told Eric that there were none for him to find.

'What happened?' Eric said.

'The old cow ...' Sandra Saxby muttered. 'She sold the bloody farm.'

'Sold it? To whom?'

They both stared at him for a long moment. Then Jack Saxby's head dropped again. 'To my father Amos,' he said.

Jack Saxby's face had a drawn, hunted look that was not matched by the expression on his wife's face. Eric felt sorry for him: it was clear that his mother's sale of the farm to Amos Saxby had been a bitter blow, not merely because of the act itself but because of its unexpectedness. It was like a betrayal: his mother had told him she would look after him: she had prepared the ground with a very favourable proposal, and it must have been a tremendous shock to him that she had behaved in this manner. Eric suspected the wound lay deep, for it seemed as though no previous discussion had taken place. But Sandra Saxby had been not so much shocked as humiliated, according to her lights. Her features expressed outrage, a vicious anger that had not been dissipated since hearing of the transaction.

'When did this sale and conveyance take place?' Eric asked.

Saxby shrugged. 'About a year ago. I ... I just got to hear about it.'

'From whom?'

Jack Saxby shrugged again, but made no reply.

'Was no explanation given to you?'

'Not a word.'

Eric Ward stared at the copy of the option to purchase signed by Ellen Saxby. It was still within the ten-year period ...

14

'The thing I want to know, Mr Ward, can she do that? Can she sell Holton Hill Farm to my father and make that piece of paper worthless?'

'Won't your father honour the option?'

Jack Saxby looked angry as his wife snorted in derision. He shook his head.

'I would advise you,' Eric said, 'that in the interests of family unity it's better merely to try to persuade your father—'

'He won't even see me,' Jack Saxby said. 'Refuses to discuss it. Said I'd been prying into his affairs and I could go to hell.'

'Stronger language than that,' Sandra Saxby announced bitterly.

'Well ...'

'Can he do it?' Saxby demanded. 'Can he refuse to go with the option now the land is his?'

Eric rose to his feet and walked across to his bookshelves. He took down the copy of *Halsbury's Statutes,* volume 27. He began to browse through the volume as he murmured, 'I don't think you need to worry too much, Mr Saxby, from the legal point of view.'

'How do you mean?'

'In 1925 an Act was passed called the Land Charges Act. The purpose of it was to make sure that people who had an interest — a legal interest or an equitable interest — in land, couldn't be cheated out of that interest. The idea is that it's no good the buyer of land saying he didn't *know* about the interest because the seller didn't tell him: the interest is registered as a charge against the land and so the buyer is bound by it whether he knew of it or not.'

'Amos knew about it all right,' Sandra Saxby snapped.

'Yes, but his knowledge, or lack of it, is irrelevant.' Eric checked the statute book. 'Yes, here we are. The option to purchase is registerable as an estate contract under section 13 of the Act. You're protected, Mr Saxby.'

'How do you mean, protected? If she's sold the land, and my father refuses—'

'He can't refuse. He has no choice. He will have taken conveyance of Holton Hill Farm subject to implied notice of the land charge. That means he takes the farm *subject to the option to purchase.*'

'A court of law would make him carry it out?'

Eric nodded.

'We've got the old bastard,' Sandra Saxby said in triumph. There was no triumph in Jack Saxby's face: rather, he still showed a mingled sadness and lack of understanding.

'But if I may offer one piece of advice, again,' Eric suggested.

'Yes?'

'It would be better if you kept it out of the courtroom. Litigation causes bitterness when it's been between members of a family. The kind of wounds that never heal.'

'He won't carry out the option without,' Sandra Saxby said.

'I would still suggest—'

Jack Saxby stared at his wife. He shook his head. 'Sandra's right. But I'll have another try at the old man, and speak to my mother. But I don't think it'll work. And if it doesn't ... we'll go to law.' He stared at Eric. 'Will you act for us, then?'

'If that's what you would want,' Eric said.

* * *

After Jack and Sandra Saxby had gone Eric Ward stood staring out of the window for a while, thinking. He felt sorry for Jack Saxby: it was clear that the distance that had now arisen between him and his mother was as hurtful to him as the actual conveyance of Holton Hill Farm to Amos Saxby. The family was being torn apart and Jack Saxby did not know why. The same emotions obviously did not plague Sandra Saxby: she had little or no regard for either of her parents-in-law: her major emotion at the end of the interview had been triumphant delight, and not only at the possibility of purchasing the farm — the mainspring of her delight was in having the chance to humble Amos Saxby.

Her relationship with her husband was also of interest to Eric. He would not have characterized Jack Saxby as a weak man, yet his wife showed an open contempt for him at times. She did not dominate him, but Eric had no doubt that she would get her own way in situations that really mattered to her. Even so, her bile against Amos and Ellen Saxby had spilled over towards her husband, and there was little doubt but that relationships would suffer whatever the result of the pressure brought to bear upon old Amos Saxby.

Eric returned to his desk and picked up the manila folders. He was about to call Philippa to remove them when he decided to check again the file index. There were four entries after 1946, the last file held. He read them again.

1969: Conveyance of Holton Hill Farm to Ellen Saxby
1969: Conveyance of Eastgate Farm to Samuel Saxby
1974: Option to purchase Holton Hill Farm
1980: Brief to counsel re Eastgate Farm right of way.

The last annotation, regarding Eastgate Farm, was in Paul Francis's hand. Eric grimaced, looked again at the entries. At least he knew what two of the files were about now — the conveyance to Ellen Saxby and the later option to purchase. But it was as well Jack Saxby had his own copy of the option — it was important that the missing files be located. He decided he would ask Philippa to make another check to make sure they weren't in the stack-room upstairs. He bundled the existing files together and headed for the door.

It opened before he reached it.

Joseph Francis smiled at him benignly. 'Ah, Eric,' he purred. 'Everything sorted out?'

Eric hesitated. 'Not exactly. A family squabble among the Saxbys, but I don't think it will come to much. I doubt if we'll be further involved — not if they've got any sense, at least.'

'Lawyers make their reputations — and their money — because people have no sense,' Joseph said, and smiled again. 'So, no problem then?'

Eric waved the folders in his hand. 'These are the Saxby files. I still think we'd better locate the missing ones, just in case: it seems they may well relate to what Jack Saxby came to see me about this morning.'

'Fine, fine, I'll ring Paul as I said, this evening, and we'll see if he's got any recollection about what might have happened to them. Meanwhile, if you're not too busy there's something else I'd like you to take on. A commercial matter, bit of employment law thrown in, I'm sure you can handle it.' He raised the file in his hand, waved it vaguely and then set it down on Eric Ward's desk.

'What is it?'

'Stoneleigh Enterprises. They've asked us to undertake the contractual aspects of their Seaham proposals. Came our way through a dinner I attended at the club last week. Not all my junketing proves fruitless, hey?'

Eric smiled. 'I never said it did, Joseph.'

'Well, no, not in my hearing anyway.' Joseph Francis adjusted his immaculate cuff. 'Take it on, there's a good chap. I'm a bit rusty on some of the items there. It could mean some hefty fees for us, though — conveyancing as well. You ... er ... you come across Stoneleigh at all before?'

'No.'

'The Honourable Antony Stoneleigh. Lord Franleigh's youngest boy. Charmin' fellow, and got his head screwed on too. Good, sound business sense; flair; acumen; bit of get up and go. Yes, charmin', and intelligent.'

'I'll take a look at the file as soon as I can.'

'Do that, my boy, do that.'

* * *

Eric Ward drove up to Lindisfarne that following weekend. It was a number of years since he had done the tourist bit, checking the tide times, crossing the causeway at low tide and then walking through the ruins of the abbey, strolling along the grassy headland and listening to the high scream of the gulls. In the afternoon he made his way southwards along the coastline to Craster, and after a light lunch walked as far as Dunstanburgh Castle, as dramatic on the headlands as it was when Turner had sketched and painted it so many times.

It was a windswept day with a faint hazy sun and the air was sharp and invigorating. He had hoped that the cobwebs would be blown from his brain, a clarity of thought achieved to match the crisp sea light, but it didn't happen: his mind still revolved around the insoluble problem. Insoluble, because the outcome depended so much upon chance. There was a *chance* that the operation would be successful, but Mr Callaghan had been so careful in his choice of words and refusal to advise that Ward's thoughts were directed towards what he guessed would be the more logical outcome: blindness.

It was coming anyway, he knew that. But not yet, not for a while, maybe a few years yet. He knew that, fierce as the pain was, it was a pain he could handle and live with. The helplessness of blindness was another matter.

The weekend, which should have been a time for rest, only left him tired and jaded on the Monday morning when he returned to the office.

He had a full day. There were several conveyancing matters to be dealt with in the morning, and a brief to counsel to prepare. Two lengthy phone calls about a mining lease and a subsidence claim against the National Coal Board whittled his morning away, and in the afternoon he was interviewing a lady about a matrimonial matter when Philippa rang him. The lady facing Eric across his desk, clutching a tear stained handkerchief to her lips, was in a state of some distress and Eric was trying to deal with the twin difficulties of calming her down and advising her to take positive steps against her husband when Philippa interrupted him. The interruption irritated him.

'Please, Philippa, I said no calls.'

'The caller was insistent and I—'

'Who is it?'

'It's the man you saw last week — Mr Saxby. He said he wanted to speak to you very urgently.'

The lady in front of Eric dissolved into a fresh flood of bitter tears.

'No, I'm sorry, Philippa,' Eric said in desperation. 'I can't speak to him now. Get his phone number and I'll ring him back as soon as I can.'

'All right, Mr Ward, I'm sorry, Mr Ward.'

Eric put the phone down and got on with the task of mollifying, and driving, the distraught lady in his room.

It was three o'clock before he was free of her, and Philippa brought him in a cup of tea between appointments. She put the cup down on his desk and smiled brightly. 'I told Mr Saxby what you said, but he said he couldn't be contacted by phone this afternoon.'

'Did he leave a message?'

'Oh yes, I'll just get it for you.'

Philippa returned with the slip of paper a few minutes later. Eric put down his cup of tea and stared at it for several long seconds. 'Is it all right, Mr Ward?'

'Philippa, I'm afraid you're going to have to cancel all my appointments for the rest of the afternoon. See if Mr James can take on some of them.'

Eric spent the next twenty minutes on the phone. Yes, he realized it was not the usual method to search; yes, he accepted that a written application was more sensible and more useful in that it fixed a date and time. Nevertheless, the matter was urgent.

Finally he persuaded the clerk at the other end of the phone. Eric then waited, a sick feeling in the pit of his stomach. At four-fifteen the phone rang. It was a confirmation of what he had feared — the accuracy of the statement made by Jack Saxby over the phone to Philippa. Eric stared again at the brief message.

Mr Saxby says to tell you that the option was never registered.

* * *

Eric glared in frustration at Joseph Francis, sitting calmly behind his desk. 'But don't you see what this means?'

'An oversight—'

'I don't think you've got the picture clearly yet. For God's sake, don't you see we're in trouble? Look at the index for the Saxby files. It was Francis, Shaw and Elder who were acting for the Saxbys. It was this firm that drew up the option to purchase. Now you know damned well that the very next step any solicitor takes is to make sure that the option would be registered as an estate contract under the Land Charges Act. The bloody thing is all but worthless, otherwise, against an innocent purchaser. It was never registered, and now there's been a further transaction!'

'Even so—'

'Joseph, this is important! I've now spoken again to Jack Saxby. His wife had to drag him off the farm to speak to me. He's upset, mad as hell. And don't you realize he could turn against the firm?'

Joseph Francis eyed Eric coolly. 'You are suggesting that Saxby might suggest we were ... a ... negligent?'

'Damn right I am.'

'It would never be worth his while. The Law Society would not countenance—'

'Joseph, he wouldn't have to go to the Law Society — and it certainly *would* be worth his while. Look, under that option to purchase he would be entitled to buy Holton Hill Farm for *three thousand pounds*. The true value of the farm at present prices is *forty thousand quid!* Now he could argue like this: if the option had been registered he could have enforced it against his father in spite of the sale, but because it wasn't registered, as a result of the negligence of Francis, Shaw and Elder, it can't be enforced. He's lost thirty-seven thousand pounds, if my maths is correct. He could take us straight to court, and as a partner in the firm I wouldn't be happy at having such a judgment against us!'

Joseph Francis had paled, and his tongue flickered nervously over his thin lips. 'Let me see that file index again.'

He stared at it as though mesmerized for several minutes, and then he rose and began to pace around the room, his head slightly bent, his eyes hooded.

'You think he'd take us to court?'

'Wouldn't you, in his place?'

Again Joseph Francis paced the room. The silence grew heavy. Suddenly the senior partner stopped in his tracks. He swivelled, to stare at Eric.

'Who did the conveyance of the farm to Amos Saxby?'

'Not us.'

'But who?'

Eric shrugged. 'I've no idea. Jack Saxby was a bit vague about the whole thing. But why do you ask? I've no evidence that the property *has* been conveyed, but if it has we're in trouble.'

Joseph Francis stared at Eric; his eyes were glittering and it was as though he hardly saw his junior partner. Eric was once again aware of the keen legal brain that the old man possessed. He waited. Suddenly, surprisingly, Joseph Francis smiled. It was not a pleasant smile.

'Let's play a game for a moment, Eric. Let's pretend you're old Amos Saxby.'

'I don't see—'

'Bear with me, dear boy. Now then, shall we assume that Amos — that is, you — has the intention of taking the conveyance from his wife?'

'That's hardly a wild assumption.'

'How much would he pay for it?'

Eric stared, surprised. 'How on earth would I know?'

'You're not playing the game, dear boy. Put yourself in old Saxby's place. How much would you pay for Holton Hill Farm? Forty thousand?'

Eric Ward shrugged helplessly. 'So much would depend ... but if I were buying it from my wife, then, I suppose, unless it was a transaction designed to make some tax saving of some kind, well, I imagine I'd pay ... as little as possible.'

'How little?'

Eric shook his head. 'Really, that's impossible to answer. And your question is pointless.'

'Is it?' There was a cold gleam in Joseph Francis's eyes as he resumed his pacing. 'You should know me better than that, young man. Think. What if old Amos Saxby did not pay his wife the actual value of the farm? What if he paid a very small sum — as is perhaps quite possible?' His smile was little more than a wolfish grimace. 'Well, Eric?'

'It won't work, Joseph.'

'What won't work, dear boy?'

Eric marched across to the bookshelves, ran his finger along the volumes of the All England Law Reports. 'I know what you're driving at. You're suggesting that if it can be shown that the price paid under the conveyance for Holton Hill Farm was inadequate—'

'An unfair and unreasonable value by way of consideration,' Joseph said, nodding.

'—then the protection given by the law to Amos Saxby, as a result of the non-registration of the option to purchase, is lost.'

'He would then be forced to take the farm subject to the option to purchase after all.'

'Not on, Joseph.' Eric shook his head. 'Not on. Here.' He handed to the senior partner the third volume of the 1978 reports. 'I've already looked at the possibility. Check on *Midland Bank Trust Company v Green*. It was held in that case that the conveyance effected a genuine passing of the legal estate, for money or money's worth, *in spite of the inadequacy of the price paid.*'

Joseph Francis ignored the proffered volume. He turned away, paced the room once more, locking his hands behind his back. 'Who knows?' he said. 'Maybe Homer nodded in that case. My lawyer's instinct suggests to me there's an arguable case, a questionable issue in those facts. It's something worth pursuing.'

'Joseph, the precedent—'

'I said I think it's worth pursuing.'

The silence grew between them. The sunlight filtering through the window picked out the gleaming gold titles on the standard blue binding of the law reports on the shelf. Ward stared at them, waiting. After a few seconds, Joseph went abruptly back to his desk and sat down. Eric waited, but the senior partner said nothing. He merely picked up a silver paperknife and began toying with it. At last Eric said, quietly, 'Just what are you suggesting, Joseph?'

'Discussion.' The sharp eyes were hooded, the voice carefully modulated. 'Just a little further ... investigation of the facts.'

'I think you're proposing more than that.'

'If the facts are supportive.'

'You can't be serious, Joseph. It's a client's money we're talking about. It would be unethical to suggest to Jack Saxby that he should sue his father, attempt to overturn this conveyance, when the law says that he doesn't stand a chance!'

Joseph Francis looked up. His mouth was tense and a nerve flickered in his cheek. 'Let's not talk about ethics at this stage, dear boy,' he said coldly. 'And let's not run before we learn to walk. I'm saying we should undertake certain further investigation on behalf of Jack Saxby. I'm suggesting that *if* the facts warrant it, we then advise Jack Saxby that he *might* have a case—'

'But—'

Joseph Francis raised an elegant hand. 'Please. You know as well as I, Eric, that most arguments of this kind, family squabbles, never get to court. They're settled, dealt with, not exactly amicably, but at least *settled*. It's my opinion that if we do some digging, the facts we find will put enough of a scare into Amos Saxby to make him settle. I think he'll either agree to the exercise of the option, or else compensate his son Jack for its loss. Jack Saxby should be grateful enough to us then.'

'And if it isn't settled?'

Sunlight flashed on the silver blade in Joseph Francis's hands. 'That's a decision for another day.'

'I don't like it, Joseph.'

The senior partner in Francis, Shaw and Elder smiled. 'You don't have to. It's my decision — though you, naturally, will be handling the matter. The first thing you must now do is to check upon the accuracy of Jack Saxby's statement. Ensure the conveyance has actually been completed. Then, you'll need to find out what the purchase price was. A chat with Amos Saxby's lawyer should be enough. If he's got any sense he'll see the possibilities. Then, if the conveyance *has* been duly completed, we can advise Jack Saxby to issue a formal notice to exercise the option granted to him by Ellen Saxby. That'll put the cat among the pigeons.'

'And if the parents don't comply with the notice?'

'They'll comply ... or settle. If we scare them enough.' Joseph stared at Eric Ward, and his glance was calculating. 'Be realistic, Eric. All we're doing is protecting the interests of a client.'

Eric held his glance for several seconds.

Slowly he shook his head. 'No. That's not it, Joseph. It's not Jack Saxby you're protecting, but Francis, Shaw and Elder. You're hoping that if we can reverse this situation, con Amos Saxby with our threats of action, make him undertake the option to purchase, it'll divert Jack Saxby's attention from the fact that he could bring a negligence claim against our firm.'

'You're over-reacting, Eric,' Joseph Francis said smoothly. 'Nothing I've said leads to that conclusion—'

'No,' Eric Ward agreed, 'nothing, as far as it goes. Advice, a bit of pressure on Amos Saxby, all right ... it's all in the interests of Jack Saxby, to give him the right to buy Holton Hill Farm. But if it goes any further than that, if we then issue a writ—'

'Yes?'

'We'd be issuing a writ in a claim we'd be bound to lose, according to precedent. And that, in my view, would be near to sharp practice.'

'Unethical ...' Joseph Francis murmured. 'Sharp practice ... You really are getting over-excited, dear boy.'

'I can't go along with a situation whereby we persuade a client to enter hopeless litigation just to try to cover up our own negligence.'

The senior partner's tones were soothing. 'But nothing's *happened,* yet; nothing's been proved; no facts properly garnered. Let's look at it, shall we? Decisions, they can come later. So ... better get on to it right away, don't you think?'

Eric hesitated, glowering at Joseph Francis. Uncertainty gripped him; maybe there was something in what the senior partner was saying; maybe the accusations Eric had made were unjust. His own legal judgment could be clouded by the pressures, both physical and mental, that disturbed him.

* * *

But later sitting alone in his office as evening drew on, he still felt he was right. Joseph Francis was an old hand at the legal niceties: he was wrapping up this package very convincingly. But there was still no gainsaying the motives behind it: they were not to help Jack Saxby, they were the erection of a smoke screen to hide the culpability of Francis, Shaw and Elder in their non-registration of the option to purchase.

Eric could not legitimately refuse to undertake what the senior partner had requested: a further investigation on Jack Saxby's behalf into the circumstances of the conveyance of Holton Hill Farm. But it still left a bitter taste in his mouth, and he was still faced with the difficulty of perhaps having to make a decision, later, if Amos Saxby had paid only a nominal sum for the farm. It was certainly possible, Eric knew that. And he also knew that in such circumstances Joseph Francis would want the issue pressed — even though it was one that would be thrown out of court.

Another decision to be put off.

Eric ran his hand over his eyes. He knew his eyelids would be red-rimmed, a combination of tiredness and anxiety, the waiting for the first flicks of pain in his eyeballs.

An immense depression washed over him. He rose, picked up his briefcase and locked the office door behind him, last to leave. He paused, irresolutely, then on impulse decided not to make his way back home to the cottage at Wylam. He put his briefcase in his car and then walked towards the city centre.

It was quiet enough as he walked along Clayton Street. He turned into the Swallow Hotel, made his way up to the lounge bar, needing a drink. He drank little now, and kept no liquor at the cottage. His illness responded badly to alcohol, but he could take an occasional drink without any serious effects and the interview with Joseph Francis combined with the decision facing him now left him needing a stiff whisky.

He entered the lounge bar, hardly noticing the small group seated just inside the doors. Then he heard the voice.

'Eric Ward!'

He stopped, turned, stared at her.

It was Ann Morcomb.

CHAPTER 2

He remembered vividly the first time he had seen her. She had come riding down through the trees on a magnificent black mare, picking her way along the narrow track with an elegant, practised ease. At their introduction he had been aware of her warmth, the regularity of her features, her confidence and social grace. Over the next days she had returned to his mind with a surprising regularity until he had dismissed her from his thoughts, a woman twenty years younger than he.

But events had thereafter thrown them together, and there had been the accident of their meeting at the burned-out ruins of Seddon Burn Hall. It was on that day he had first seen the red-gold tints in her hair, and felt the first lift of tension between them, unexplained, to him inexplicable. Until the last day at Sedleigh Hall, when he realized what had arisen between them and, ill, with the void of twenty years between them, he had walked away from her, denying the fact that he had fallen in love with her, unwilling to accept that she could be in love with him.

Now, two years later, he felt the quick movement of his blood as he saw her again, rising from her chair to greet him as he remained rooted to the spot, aware that for him nothing had changed.

She came forward, holding out her hand. She was smiling, and if there was something in her eyes he could not read it. 'Hello, Eric. It's good to see you.'

Her grasp was warm and friendly; he tried to inject impersonality into his and the smile was in her eyes too. She had always been a perceptive young woman.

Eric hesitated. 'I ... I heard your father ... Lord Morcomb had died. I'm sorry.'

Half-forgotten shadows suddenly darkened her glance and she put her head on one side, made a small gesture of resignation. 'It was hardly unexpected. And at the end it was quite painful for him. In so many ways.'

'A happy release,' Eric said inanely, aware that there were forbidden grounds on which he must not tread. 'The estates ... everything is going well?' He had advised her what needed to be done two years ago.

She nodded, now. 'Yes, I changed the shares portfolio as you suggested and we managed to block the outsiders. I now use an investment manager here in Newcastle and we've got a good accountant.' Her eyes met his. 'There's been no further need of lawyers once the will was dealt with and probate obtained. I thought you would have ... I mean ...'

'No, Joseph handled it.' Eric managed a tight smile. 'You know, he always likes to deal with the really important clients himself.' He hesitated, 'Well ...'

'You've come in for a drink?' Her eyes were on him, searching, watchful.

'It's been a long day,' he said, afraid to betray his feelings.

'If you're alone, and expecting no one, why don't you join us?'

Eric Ward glanced past her to the two men who were sitting in the corner, awaiting her return. 'I'm not sure—'

'Don't be so stuffy.' She grinned at him mischievously. 'Come and meet them — you might even pick up some business from them.'

Eric had no further opportunity to resist as she laid a slim hand on his arm and tugged at his sleeve, gently drawing him towards the table.

'This is Eric Ward,' she announced. 'A solicitor friend of mine who sorted out a few problems for Daddy and me a couple of years back — at no small cost to himself.' Her eyes flashed briefly to him but he could not, or did not want to, read what they said. 'And this is Antony Stoneleigh — the *Honourable* Antony Stoneleigh, I should say.'

'I get no chance to be other,' Stoneleigh said, grinning at her. Eric shook hands and then turned to the other man. 'And this is Colin Saxby,' Anne announced.

'Then there's no new business here for me,' Eric said, smiling as he shook hands with Colin Saxby.

'New business?' Antony Stoneleigh asked, raising his eyebrows. Eric glanced at him. The youngest son of Lord Franleigh had impressed Joseph Francis and physically Eric could understand why. Stoneleigh was six feet tall, impeccably dressed in a grey, pin-striped suit and broad-shouldered, lean-waisted. His hair was long, fair, and fashionably cut and his skin was tanned, his grey eyes friendly, his handclasp warm. He gave an impression of easy charm, allied to strength; there was a determined line to his jaw and Eric guessed his mouth would on occasions display a hint of ruthlessness. He looked a capable young man, still with horizons to reach for, and the power and capability to reach them.

'Just a joke,' Anne said. 'But ...' She looked quizzically at Eric as she sat down.

'I have just been given a file on Stoneleigh Enterprises,' Eric explained.

'You're with Francis, Shaw and Elder?' Stoneleigh queried. 'Ah, I see. Yes, I met Joseph Francis. I was impressed with him. A wily old bird ... no fool.'

'A good lawyer,' Eric agreed.

Colin Saxby stood up and suggested he get a round of drinks; Eric accepted a whisky and soda and Saxby went across to the bar.

'So, what do you think of our little enterprise?' Stoneleigh asked, his grey eyes fixed on Eric.

'I'm afraid I can pass no opinion as yet,' Eric replied. 'The way business has been going the last few days I've had no time to take a look at the file.'

Anne Morcomb laughed. 'Well, you'd better take a look at it, if only to advise me.'

'That's not fair,' Antony Stoneleigh protested. 'If Mr Ward is acting for me, it's not right that you should go to him for advice. Professional ethics, isn't it, Mr Ward?'

Eric smiled and shrugged. 'It depends what Anne's interest is, I suppose. But in principle, I agree; I couldn't talk to her about your business if I'm acting for you. As Mr Stoneleigh says — not ethical.'

'Stuffy,' Anne Morcomb said mockingly. 'I thought we were friends. Besides, I saw you first.'

There was a subtle undercurrent in the last remark that caused Antony Stoneleigh to glance at Eric Ward; slightly discomfited, Eric turned to Anne. 'Just what is your problem, anyway?'

'Ah, well, it's the problem all wealthy young women face, I suppose. Here I am, poor little rich girl, heiress to considerable Northumberland estates, at the mercy of every presentable young man—'

'My *dear*,' Stoneleigh said mockingly.

'—every *almost* presentable young man, all of whom are merely after my money.'

'Your money *first*, my dear, but thereafter ...'

It was now Eric Ward's turn to sense the vibrations that underlined the man's mocking tone. Stoneleigh's eyes were on Anne, and the admiration in them was frank and open. The words were uttered in a spirit of badinage but there was an underlying seriousness in them that made Eric realize these two could be more than merely friends, and questions might already have been asked.

And perhaps answered. The thought made his flesh suddenly cold.

'Well, let's stick to the money,' Anne said, laughing. 'Fact is, Eric, this shady character here wants me to sink some of my ill-gotten gains into Stoneleigh Enterprises. Now then, what should I do? Advise me.'

Eric shrugged. 'I'm in no position to advise. I don't even know yet what the business involves.'

Antony Stoneleigh turned to him; there was a gleam of real excitement in his eyes, the enthusiasm of a committed man. 'It's considerable, Mr Ward. And important for the North-East.'

'Antony regards himself as a Geordie, in spite of his London home and his Cambridge accent,' Anne mocked.

'I'll ignore that,' Stoneleigh said. 'You'll be aware, Mr Ward, that my family have strong northern connections. Our fortunes, so to speak, have been built upon mining interests on the north-east coast.'

Albeit as absent landowners, Eric thought.

'The mining days are over now, of course,' Stoneleigh was continuing, 'and that means we have no real connections with the area now, other than historically. But, well, I still feel roots are important ... Anyway, the fact is, I feel quite strongly about the principle of bringing work back into the area, and developing Seaham again, in the way I know it can be developed.'

'Why Seaham?' Eric asked.

'Communications — the A19 spine road running north and south, with easy access to Sunderland, Newcastle and Teesside. Housing: the new town at Peterlee and development grants. Land availability ... there are lots of reasons.'

'And I shouldn't mock, I know,' Anne Morcomb said. 'Ah, here's Colin.'

Colin Saxby set down the drinks. 'When you said no business, I got the impression you included me, Mr Ward.'

'Well, our firm already acts for the Saxby family. I presume you're ... Jack Saxby's brother.'

'That's right.' But he did not look much like him, Eric Ward thought. He would be a head taller, and slimmer, without the depth of chest, and rather smoother of manner. Colin Saxby held himself with a military bearing and sported a small moustache: like Stoneleigh, he seemed at ease in company in a way Jack Saxby never would be, and like Stoneleigh, he projected an image of confidence that would serve him well in business.

But the Honourable Antony Stoneleigh had started talking about his pet project, and would not now be gainsaid or interrupted.

It was, he insisted, a project that would not only bring work into the area but one that could bring a great deal of prestige to the country. His family had built its fortune on coal, some of it mined in drifts that had run out under the sea and stained the north-east coastline with black dust. His own project was also a mining one, but directly on the sea-bed.

'You see, the ocean floor is rich in minerals. Scattered along the bed, buried in slurry, are nodules — small, black, rocklike objects which contain concentrations of manganese, copper, nickel and cobalt. The object of the exercise is to lift those nodules to the surface, transfer them ashore and extract the minerals. You see how big the whole thing could be? I'm talking, eventually, of a pipeline to the shore near Seaham, the building of a refinery, and within ten years an operation that could be producing a minimum extraction of three million tons of nodules a year. Maybe ten thousand tons a day.'

'And just how would you get the nodules to the surface?' Eric asked.

'You remember *Glomar Explorer?* The ship used by the CIA in 1974 in that unsuccessful shot they had at raising a Soviet submarine from the ocean floor north of Hawaii? Well, the whole thing's been developed much further now and a similar ship would be used, but one which would combine two operations. The first would be the jibs and derricks on deck joining up and letting down maybe three miles of steel pipe. The second, in the centre of the hull, is a huge well with steel doors opening towards the sea-bed. That's used for letting down the claw-equipped submarine recovery vehicle.'

He launched into an explanation of the process. Eric watched and noted the animation of his features, the conviction in his eyes as he explained how the bottom miner — a cross between an underwater tank and a vacuum cleaner — would move as deeply as 18,000 feet, the crawler scouring the sea-bed sucking up nodule slurry and forcing it into the steel pipe to the ship. On the ship the potato-sized nodules would be washed in large sieves and made ready for transfer, in commercial operations, to shore-based refineries.

'Don't get me wrong,' Stoneleigh insisted. 'This isn't pie in the sky; it isn't even new. The technology is here: there are three international consortiums engaged in such mining developments. The Japanese are into it, so are the Americans and the Canadians. We've known about the nodules since 1873 when they were first discovered in an oceanographic survey by HMS *Challenger*. But the activity is all elsewhere, in the Pacific mainly, south-east of Hawaii.'

'The capital investment needed would be enormous.' Eric said.

'That's why it's up to international consortiums.'

'And your operation?'

'Is only the first step. A survey.' Stoneleigh's eyes were cold for a few minutes as he explained how the British Government had been slow to recognize the potential in bottom mining. When he had spoken to grey-faced civil servants in Whitehall they had raised objections: unproved systems, disputed results, ecological attitudes and the damage that could be done to sea life. And there was the political matter of the controls being pressed, through the suggested establishment of an International Sea-bed Authority.

'If we wait for that,' Stoneleigh said, 'we'd wait until the turn of the century.'

But the final civil service card had been the evidence of the existence of nodules in commercial quantities. It was an answer that had determined Stoneleigh to act on his own.

'They won't pump in the money till there's evidence; all right, that means it's got to be done as a commercial venture. I can get hold of the expertise; I can get hold of the equipment. Six months test dragging; a feasibility study by appropriate people; locations, sites, refinery possibilities, communications ... that's the business, Mr Ward. The business, the prospects, the chance of reinvigorating the North-East, showing Whitehall where they get off and, for the investors, the chances later of huge — and I mean huge — profits.'

Anne was smiling at Eric, a little quizzically. 'He sounds convincing, doesn't he?'

'I ought to.' Stoneleigh laughed delightedly. 'I've got the confidence of knowledge. I've been to the States; I've seen the Pacific operations; I know what I'm talking about. The nodules will be here in commercial quantities and I can put back into the North-East what my family — and others — took out over the centuries.'

'A sense of mission, no less,' Anne added drily.

'Well, he's convinced me, at least,' Colin Saxby said. He sipped at his gin and tonic and slipped a finger against his sandy moustache. The skin around his eyes crinkled as he grinned. 'I think the thing's worth a gamble, and more — and Tony here's got the know-how.'

'So,' Anne asked Eric, 'should I part with some of my pin-money?'

'You could marry me instead,' Antony Stoneleigh said swiftly.

Something moved in Eric Ward's chest. 'I don't know how to advise,' he said.

'On the investment,' Anne said coolly, 'or the proposal?'

With difficulty, Eric managed a smile but turned to Colin Saxby, avoiding the implications in the question. 'You in farming also?' he asked.

'Like my brothers?' Colin Saxby laughed; it had a booming confidence about it and yet there was a hollow ring to it as well. 'Started that way, but sold Brookfield Farm last year. Not really cut out, you see.'

'How do you mean?'.

Colin Saxby furrowed his brow. 'You'll be involved with Saxby family affairs so you'll know the general picture. Money in the background; grandfather Saxby with successful landholdings; father Amos carrying on and making his own way in life. There's a kind of tradition, isn't there, a sort of patterned existence about it all? Trouble is, if you get out, see places, meet people, your ideas change. The pattern changes shape.'

'Is that what happened to you?'

Colin Saxby nodded. 'That's right. In a nutshell, I joined the Army. Saw service in Cyprus; Northern Ireland. Came back, end of commission — I was a major in the infantry — and then everything's a bit out of kilter, know what I mean? Of course, Amos had it all planned out; he'd always had it fixed. He made Brookfield Farm over to me and I ran it for a few years. But the old heart wasn't in it, don't you know? Couldn't see myself ploughing the same old furrow year in, year out. The Army, it gave me a sense of adventure; farming couldn't satisfy that. So ... I sold Brookfield Farm.'

'Your father can't have been terribly happy about that.' Anne murmured.

Colin Saxby shrugged. 'Didn't have much say in it, though, did he? All right, maybe he wouldn't have sold me the farm for a song if he'd known I wasn't going to make a go of it, but that's not the point. He was providing for my future and I was grateful; but it wasn't what I wanted. I'm thirty-eight now and I've time yet to do something other than farming. In fact, I've found what I want to do; it's why I've thrown in with Tony here.'

'Never know,' Stoneleigh drawled mockingly, 'Colin might even end up driving the blasted bottom miner.'

Saxby laughed. 'Well, it'd be more exciting than herding cows.' He hesitated, then glanced at Eric Ward. 'You say you're acting for the Saxbys. Amos buying more land, is he?'

'It's not Amos Saxby we're acting for at the moment,' Eric replied after a moment, unwilling to say more. But Colin Saxby was staring at him thoughtfully.

Eric turned away to say something to Anne, but Saxby suddenly said, 'It's Jack, is it?'

Eric opened his mouth, but then, with a swift glance at the others, said nothing.

Colin Saxby sighed. 'Family trouble,' he said. 'Worst kind, isn't it, always the worst kind. But I could see it coming, you know; it was always on the cards.' He looked up to Antony Stoneleigh. 'You're a youngest son; you know maybe the way things can be. There are three of us, you see — Sam, he's the oldest, then me, and then Jack. Solid lad, Jack, always cut out to be a farmer. All he ever wanted.' He grimaced. 'Old Amos, he knew that. Always seemed fond of Jack, for that matter — saw good farming stock in him. Still ...' He was silent for a few moments, then shrugged. 'Anyway, it's Jack who's ended up with the wrong end of the stick.'

'What's happened?' Antony Stoneleigh asked. Eric shifted uncomfortably in his seat; he did not consider Colin Saxby should discuss family matters in this way, but after all, that was his decision.

'Well,' Colin Saxby continued, 'Amos had inherited a couple of farms which he and my mother worked and built up. But, two farms, three sons. Sam came first, as the eldest, of course. He was given a tenancy of Eastgate Farm, proved himself and then Amos transferred it to him, for a song. That was the pattern, you see: as Amos got older, near retirement, he'd make it over. I was over in Aldershot when he rang me about Brookfield Farm but I said I wasn't coming back to a tenancy, so when I came out of the Army he conveyed it to me.' Saxby glanced at Eric, smiling apologetically. 'Don't think your firm was involved. No fees there. Anyway, that was two of us fixed for life, sort of.'

'And that left the youngest brother,' Anne Morcomb murmured sympathetically.

'Well, it seemed as though it would be all right. Amos had the two farms, but my mother, Ellen, she'd been given a property under the will of her cousin, Frank Jennings. So,

37

there was a sort of understanding. And that was the way it was worked. My mother gave the lease of the farm — Holton Hill Farm — that was in her name, to Jack. And things have been fine, until recently. I'm not certain what's been going on ...' He glanced at Eric as though expecting a comment, but when there was none he shrugged. 'All I do know is that Amos and Jack aren't quite seeing eye to eye at the moment.'

There was a short silence, embarrassed at the edges. Eric knew more of the facts than the others but he felt exposed, as they did, to the rattling of skeletons that were best left undisturbed.

Colin Saxby sighed. 'Anyway, as I said ... families.' He glanced at Stoneleigh. 'Youngest sons?'

'You said it.' There was a hint of mockery in Stoneleigh's grey eyes. 'But there are ways of sorting your life out. I won't succeed to the title — that's Fred's prerogative. But, hell, there are empires to build and worlds to conquer.' He flicked a glance towards Eric Ward. 'And those who get towed along with a vision, they soak up quite a bit of gravy too.'

'You really believe in this project don't you, Tony?' Anne said. There was a hint of admiration in her tone that somehow Eric resented.

'Enough to back it with every penny I've got.'

'Me too,' Colin Saxby said fervently. 'Don't get me wrong,' Antony Stoneleigh said smoothly. 'This is no reaction thing — a tyro needing to prove something. I know what I'm talking about, and if you're prepared to make an investment it'll be well spent, Anne. Though I'd still rather you'd marry me!'

He stopped abruptly as a waiter walked into the bar, hesitated, and approached them. 'Mr Stoneleigh's party?'

Antony Stoneleigh said, 'Yes.'

'Mr Saxby?'

Colin Saxby sat up. The waiter turned to him. 'We've just had a call at reception, sir. There's a request that you phone this number as soon as possible.'

Antony Stoneleigh raised his eyebrows; Saxby shrugged, made his excuses, muttering it might be something important, and then left for the telephone in the hallway.

Eric sipped at his whisky; suddenly he felt, ill at ease as though he were interrupting something. He realized it was because of the brief silence that fell; Stoneleigh, at least, would appreciate having Anne Morcomb alone. He struggled with the whisky, feeling Anne's eyes upon him. 'I think I'd better be going.'

'It was nice meeting you again, Eric,' Anne said. He stared at her for a moment, but there was nothing to say; there had been a moment at Sedleigh Hall, two years ago, when her eyes had asked questions of him, questions he was not prepared to answer then. Now, her glance was more veiled, inscrutable; she was two years older, and he was two years nearer the situation that had deterred him then.

'Yes, I expect we'll be crossing paths again,' Antony Stoneleigh said cheerfully. 'We're only months away from the blossoming of the project now and I'll certainly need to call on you to discuss the contractual details. In fact, I've got Sir John Freshfield coming up in a few weeks' time: he's got the kind of influence that can get a question asked in the Lords, so I'll need to wine and dine him a bit, to put on the pressure — right kind of pressure, you understand. Then, well, maybe Francis, Shaw and Elder will be dipping into the gravy even faster.'

'Yes, well, I've no doubt we'll be in touch.' Eric Ward struggled to finish his drink, aware again of Anne Morcomb's glance and conscious of the hint of concern demonstrated by the little line that had appeared between her eyebrows. He rose, began to murmur his goodbye.

There was someone at his elbow. It was Colin Saxby. His brow was furrowed and his mouth downturned at the corners. It was dissatisfaction rather than distress; annoyance rather than anxiety. He picked up his gin and tonic and swallowed it down in a gulp.

'I'm going to have to leave rather abruptly. Bad form and all that but ...'

'Trouble?' Antony Stoneleigh asked.

'You could say that. But why I have to be involved ...' He paused. 'You will forgive me, Anne, but I'd better get up to Morpeth as ... instructed.' He looked suddenly at Antony Stoneleigh and something seemed to pass between them, a private understanding, a reason, an acceptance that was closed to their companions. Saxby turned, then looked at Eric Ward. 'You did say Jack was consulting you?'

'Well, yes, but—'

'It's a pity he didn't leave it at that. Whatever legal advice you might have given him, he's gone charging out to my parents' home at Morpeth. There's been trouble. Arguments.'

'Not serious, I hope?' Anne asked.

'Serious enough. Amos just rang me. It's my mother.' His pale eyes dwelled briefly on Eric Ward. 'It seems she's had a stroke.'

* * *

'Your Honour, the plaintiff company has been selling washing machines and other domestic appliances and appointing salesmen, who were independent contractors. Each salesman entered into a contract with the company. Under his contract he paid over to the company, weekly, all cash received, without deduction of commission ...'

From the back of the court Eric Ward watched and listened. Paul Francis had a good voice, his diction was clear and precise, unlike many of the barristers in practice who seemed to pay little attention to what was in effect a major tool of their trade. Francis had a certain style also, which he had never been able to demonstrate as a solicitor: the little advocacy he had done in the police courts for Francis, Shaw and Elder had never allowed him to develop the kind of attack he was clearly capable of producing now.

Joseph Francis had certainly helped the fledgling in his early months at the Bar; now, Eric suspected, Paul Francis was perfectly capable of making his own way. He appeared to enjoy his court work, and it looked as though his grasp of his briefs was such that he did his homework too — which was a change from his attitude as a solicitor working with his father.

Eric glanced at his watch: it would be another hour or so till adjournment, even though Paul Francis was making his closing speech. Eric's own case was a youthful offender driving while disqualified matter, being dealt with in Court No.3 before Judge Charnley, in which the judge would be just about ready now to deliver sentence. Eric decided he had better get back into court for the decision, and then try to catch Paul Francis before the lunch adjournment.

He made his way quietly to Court No.3, nodding to familiar faces on the way, and entered just as the court was rising. The brief was held by Charlie Dawson, a barrister in his mid-fifties whom Eric had seen much of when he was in the police force, since Dawson specialized in criminal cases. Dawson raised a hand as he entered, waving him forward.

'Twelve months,' he said.

'Twelve? Bit steep, isn't it?'

'Case for appeal, I reckon,' Dawson shrugged. 'It was imposed as an aggregate sentence but I don't reckon it can stand in view of section 20 of the '61 Act. Better take up the papers for appeal: four months is nearer the mark than twelve.' He began to pick up his papers, shuffling them into a heap on the table.

'You'll be available, Charlie?'

'Always liked Court of Criminal Appeal stuff,' Dawson smiled. 'Does my fee-book no end of good. You been next door?'

'No. Dropped into Court No.1.'

'Ah yes. Paul Francis, isn't it?' Dawson eyed Eric Ward for a moment. 'He's doing well. Right decision to make, leaving the office. Er ... why did he decide to try the Bar?'

'Why do you ask?' Eric countered.

Charlie Dawson chuckled. 'All right, mind my own business. It's just curiosity, really. Paul Francis is doing well, so I should just leave it at that. It's just that ... well, I sometimes feel maybe he's a bit too ... shall we say, lax? Bit careless.'

'In handling his briefs?'

Dawson shook his head. 'No, in *getting* them. Let's say he works too hard at ... er ... making connections. Maybe it's a chip off the old block thing, hey? Old Joseph is no slouch in that direction. But Paul ... well, it's been commented on in the Bar Mess, so he ought to be a bit careful. You friendly enough to drop a word?'

'Hardly.'

'Pity ... Not that he doesn't do a good job when he's got the brief ... but one doesn't trample to get ahead. On the other hand—' he smiled ruefully — 'maybe it's just jealousy, hey? I mean, look at me. Still living by the skin of my teeth.'

'Police work was never that remunerative, Charlie.'

'But it suits me. Well, Eric ... see you in court.'

Eric followed him out, handed the papers to a legal executive from the firm and then returned to Court No.1. Paul Francis was still commanding the attention of the judge.

'So, in conclusion, Your Honour, I would add that the defendant, is in our contention, entitled to a set-off by virtue of section 31 of the Bankruptcy Act 1914 as applied by section 317 of the Companies Act 1948, and is further entitled to a lien on the money and goods in his hands ...'

As Paul Francis wound up, Eric watched the back of the briefing solicitor's head: the bald pate moved up and down in silent agreement with counsel's remarks: Tranby had always been a 'nodder', but only when he was in full agreement with counsel's performance. He was obviously happy with Paul Francis's dash in this case.

Twenty minutes later the court rose, and Eric walked outside to wait in the corridor. Francis emerged, slightly flushed, with Tranby; he caught sight of Eric and raised his hand. Eric nodded, and waited until Tranby shook hands and departed, then he met Paul Francis at the doorway.

'Congratulations,' he said.

'You were in the courtroom?'

'For a while. It went well.'

Francis smiled his pleasure, his narrow face animated. 'Well, old Tranby seems pleased. Says he wants me to meet an industrial client of his; American-based firm, located in Washington — County Durham, unfortunately, not DC!' He grinned, happy at his recent success. 'How are things with you, Eric?'

'Well enough. Bit of a problem at the moment, though, over the Saxbys.'

A frown shadowed Paul Francis's brow, and his glance flickered away as though suddenly seeking escape. 'Saxby ... yes, Dad asked me about it the other day.'

'We can't trace a couple of files. I thought that since you were the last to handle them—'

'Can't say I recall too much about them.' Francis's tone was offhand, but there was something else in his voice that betrayed a degree of uneasiness surprising to Eric. 'I mean, two or three years ago ... I told the old man, I can't really help. Don't know what'll have happened to them.'

'So you can't help?'

The tone changed again, a hint of belligerence creeping in. 'I don't know what the problem is. As far as I can make out, it's Jack Saxby who's retaining the firm, isn't it? My last dealing was with Sam Saxby—'

'Something to do with Eastgate Farm?'

'That's it. Pretty straightforward stuff, really. He'd been in possession of the farm for some years, but a dispute arose with a neighbouring landowner over wayleaves; it got as far as the County Court but then they settled. It was small beer. That's the last occasion — if not the *only* occasion — I handled Saxby matters.'

Eric stared at him. 'Who handled the option to purchase Holton Hill Farm, then? Who drew it up?'

43

'How the hell should I know?' Francis's glance was evasive. 'Look, I've got to get off to lunch — I'm meeting a possible client. If I do remember anything of assistance I'll give you a ring, but right now I'm afraid I'll have to leave you. See you, Eric.'

His step, as he walked away, seemed to contain a hint of agitation.

* * *

As he took the A1 out of Newcastle that afternoon, Eric Ward's thoughts dwelled on Paul Francis's attitude. It had been more than mere impatience at being asked about something he had dealt with more than two years previously; Eric wondered what Joseph Francis might have said to his son to cause him to be nervous at the issue arising again, with Eric.

The last annotation in the file index had been in Paul Francis's hand. It concerned the Eastgate Farm wayleave. The annotation against the option to purchase entry had been in a different hand — but it could have been one of the clerks, acting on instructions. Two assistant solicitors had left during the last five years — it could have been one of them. Eric was puzzled. Paul Francis had not noted the missing files when he had dealt with Eastgate, but he had been noted for a degree of carelessness at Francis, Shaw and Elder. Had they been missing at that time, or had they gone astray only when Paul had handled them?

He accelerated onto the dual carriageway past the Three Mile Inn, and thrust further consideration of Paul Francis from his mind. He had other things to think about, not least the kind of reception he might get at Amos Saxby's. It was a delicate mission he was embarking on: he needed to get some facts, without disclosing precisely why he needed them. If he was challenged he would have to use the writ he had ready prepared in his pocket, because although he had told Joseph Francis he was prepared to carry out only an investigation, Jack Saxby had since instructed him by phone that he was to take any steps necessary to get the option to purchase undertaken. But the writ would nevertheless remain as a weapon of last resort as far as Eric was concerned.

The line of hills rose up ahead of him: Cheviot, the border country, blue-hazed in the afternoon sky, and he recalled the occasions when he had driven out there on another legal matter, to the estates of Lord Morcomb. The landowner would have approved of the Honourable Antony Stoneleigh as a suitor for Anne's hand: good, blue, aristocratic blood. And, if he were completely objective, Eric Ward would have to admit that such a marriage would be of the right kind for her, too: she had considerable estates to manage and she needed someone with business acumen. Besides, if the Stoneleigh Enterprises project proved as successful as was hoped, the Honourable Antony would be adding considerably to the Morcomb estates in such a marriage.

The ache in his chest was merely indigestion, he insisted to himself; he had already walked away from that girl and it had been right. There would be no second chance, and even if there was ...

The signs pointed to Morpeth.

Eric drove through the archway at the entrance of the town, past the market square, and took the road winding up into the hills above. The Old Vicarage was a mile beyond the town, a rambling building all grey stone and slate, set in an acre of land and proclaiming its reason for existence with a magnificent stained-glass window set immediately above the heavy wooden door of the main entrance, lighting the staircase inside. Gravel rasped under his tyres as he drove up to the front door and parked beside the bushes at the end of the drive. As he got out he could see the gardens at the back of the old house: a vegetable plot, lawns, fruit bushes, an orchard. It had been built to accommodate a vicar who had lived in style: it suited now a farmer who was living in retirement.

45

Eric rang the bell, and waited.

The man whose footsteps echoed down the hallway and then opened the door to him was vaguely familiar. He was tall, with sandy hair and his features recalled someone else to mind. His shoulders were as broad as Jack Saxby's but his pale eyes belonged to someone else.

'Mr Saxby?' Eric ventured.

'I'm Sam Saxby.'

The eldest brother of Colin and Jack: the resemblance lay in the man Eric had met at the Swallow Hotel.

'I rang earlier,' Eric explained. 'My name's Ward, from Francis, Shaw and Elder.'

The man's mouth tightened at the corners and the glance that flickered over Eric Ward held a hint of hostility. Sam Saxby hesitated a moment, then said, 'We're not too clear what you want from us.'

'It's really a matter I wish to discuss with Mr Amos Saxby ... and Mrs Saxby, if possible.'

'My mother ... you'll understand she's been taken ill. She won't be able to see you.'

'I understand that, but my appointment with Amos Saxby will probably clear up—'

Sam Saxby stood aside abruptly. 'You'd better come in.'

The hallway was long and cool. Saxby led the way past the large kitchen on the left and turned into a sitting-room beyond. 'I'll get my father,' he said, and left. Eric admired the stone carving of the fireplace and then walked across to the tall windows with their boarded shutters. The garden beyond was bathed in sunshine and the grass glowed under the dappling branches of the orchard. When he heard the steps in the hallway he turned and Amos Saxby entered the room.

He had an old man's shoulders and a young man's eyes: his stoop was caused by his age but it left him still a tall, lean giant of a man; the piercing blue of his eyes lanced into the object of his gaze as though determined to burn out the truth. He strode rather than walked and Eric knew he would always do everything positively, and with an irresistible sense of purpose. A stereotype of a patriarch, Eric imagined: a man who would dominate his family, school his sons — and yet a man who would also have the heart and understanding to appreciate that the son who did not wish to follow in his footsteps should yet be allowed to carve out a career for himself. But Amos Saxby would allow only one chance of that kind, for he himself had never been a loser and would be the kind of individual who would not understand or accept weakness in his own children. A hard man, but probably a fair one, within his limits. Eric stared at the tanned wrinkled face under the shock of grey hair, bristling stiffly from the scalp, and introduced himself.

'Lawyers. Always been wary of 'em.' Amos Saxby humphed, walked across the room and dropped his long frame into a deep armchair. 'You've come at a bad time, young man.'

'I'm sorry ... I heard about Mrs Saxby.'

'And you come here representing my ... son.'

'Mr Jack Saxby is my client, sir, yes.'

Amos Saxby was silent for a little while. He stared at Eric Ward and his eyes were hard, blue chips of ice: tightly controlled emotions moved behind the glance and his thin lips were stretched, bared slightly over his teeth. He would be a bad man to cross, Amos Saxby, and a bitter enemy to face. Amos threw his head back suddenly and his lean neck corded as he shouted, 'Sam! You better get in here!'

Sam Saxby came in after a few moments. He stood near the door, making no attempt to sit down and Eric remained standing also as the old man's eyes glittered up at him. 'Sam was here when it happened,' Amos Saxby said.

'I—'

'This *client* of yours,' Amos sneered, 'this ... son of mine, he came blazing in here shouting about his rights. Young man, do you know anything at all about rights? In my world you don't get an entitlement to 'em just because you exist, or got a name. You *earn* 'em. You work, you build ... and you show respect. That whippersnapper ...'

47

Eric was left with a strange feeling as the old man rumbled on. He felt as though he were in a theatre, watching a stage performance, a show of power and thunder and strength, but a performance nevertheless. There was something lacking, an element of reality, as Amos Saxby spoke bitterly of his son Jack, for his eyes remained cold, not with anger, but with the ice of a banker weighing up a customer. Eric waited as the diatribe lengthened and Sam Saxby stood passively in the doorway.

'And you know what happened?' Amos Saxby was demanding. 'He had the nerve to come here, late at night, shouting the odds, complaining about the way he'd been treated, and threatening me with the law. Threatening me with *you*, young man. You,' he sneered, 'don't look so much of a threat to me.' The old man waited for a reaction; there was none from Eric, and the blue eyes glittered in satisfaction. 'So as far as I'm concerned, he and you can go to hell. Law is for lawyers and I'll have no truck with it. So you can go.'

'When I've asked a few questions, Mr Saxby, if you don't mind.'

'*I mind!* Jack came here shouting and bawling as though he already owned Holton Hill Farm — and he doesn't! *I* do! But Ellen — my wife — she couldn't stand it, and all the ranting and raving caused her to collapse. You understand, young man? My son upset his mother: she's had a stroke! So don't talk to me of laws!'

Suddenly, surprisingly, he hoisted himself out of his chair and beckoned, ordering Eric to follow him. They walked silently out of the room, Sam Saxby bringing up the rear as they climbed the broad stairs, past the stained-glass window splashing colour on the carpet, and along the wide hall landing. The door to the bedroom on the left was open: Amos Saxby marched in and then stood at the bedside. He turned to Eric. 'My wife,' he said. There was no emotion in his tone.

She was lying in the bed, her arms outside the coverlet. Her mouth drooped at one side and there was a slackness

48

about her face muscles that suggested to Eric she was probably partially paralysed as a result of the stroke. He felt a distaste well inside him at the way in which Amos Saxby had brought him up here, almost as though he were exhibiting a damaged possession, a chattel of little consequence, some value, but no real importance. Amos was staring at him as he looked at Mrs Saxby, and Eric felt the old man was waiting for something.

Ellen Saxby's eyes were alive and she too stared at Eric. He recognized the emotions that were locked in her glance: pleading, and fear.

'My wife can't speak to you,' Amos Saxby said harshly, 'and I've no desire to. You've seen; now you can go.' He did not glance at Ellen Saxby as he stumped out of the room; Eric followed as Sam Saxby closed the door behind them.

'There are still questions to be answered, Mr Saxby,' Eric insisted.

'Not by me.'

'If not here, sir, elsewhere,' Eric said quietly.

Amos Saxby stopped in the bend of the stairs. The blue of the dress of the Virgin Mary marked his face as the sun streamed through the window; the red of her kirtle touched his mouth as he smiled grimly. 'You threatening me, in my own house?'

'My client—'

'Damn your client!'

'Jack Saxby has asked me to put to you that you have behaved ... unfairly in taking the conveyance of Holton Hill Farm, in an attempt to defeat his interest.'

'*I have* defeated his interest.'

'Not necessarily.'

'Ellen conveyed the farm to me,' Amos Saxby said harshly. 'The option to purchase was not registered. The law—'

'The law is not so simple. Are you telling me you quite deliberately set out to defeat the option, knowing of its existence, by taking the conveyance, Mr Saxby?'

49

The old man hesitated, glaring at Eric. 'Don't beard me, young feller. I can bite.'

'*Was* that your motive, Mr Saxby? Because, if so, a court of law might be interested in it.'

'The law says the option is defeated. I have taken advice on the matter—'

'May I have the name of your solicitor, sir? The one who completed the transaction on your behalf?'

Amos Saxby's glance slipped past Eric to Sam, standing at the head of the stairs. Then, abruptly he turned away and marched down to the hallway. Eric followed and they stood just inside the door. 'The way out,' Amos said harshly.

'Your solicitor?' Eric pressed.

'Cranby,' Amos growled. 'The firm of Cranby and Grafton.'

Sam moved past him and opened the door.

Eric frowned. 'That's a Berwick firm, isn't it?'

Something moved in Amos Saxby's eyes and his mouth twisted. He nodded. 'Goodbye, young man.'

In the doorway, Eric said, 'You've always used our firm previously. Seems odd, going to Berwick.'

There was a cynical twist to the old man's mouth now. 'He came well recommended; a good man, well recommended.'

'Just one more thing, Mr Saxby. I gather your motives in undertaking the conveyance — after receiving legal advice from someone — are now pretty clear. But perhaps you're prepared to tell me what the purchase price of Holton Hill Farm was.'

Amos Saxby smiled broadly. 'I never believe in putting money into lawyer's pockets; I know you fellers work on a percentage basis like so many so-called *professional* people. Between a husband and wife, or any other people, I suppose, a transaction like this is just their business. And if Ellen was prepared to sell me the property for tuppence, there's not a damned thing anyone else can do about it. Isn't that so, Mr Ward?'

'That is the law, certainly,' Eric agreed.

'So I've no objection to telling you,' Amos Saxby announced triumphantly. 'So you can tell that snivelling client of yours! He's lost Holton Hill Farm to me, and he'll never get it now! And the price I paid for it? I'll tell you, so you can tell him and see him burn! Five hundred pounds, Mr Smart Lawyer. I got it for five hundred quid!'

Eric nodded. He put his hand in his pocket and pulled out the writ. 'Then you'd better also have this,' he said and turned his back on the spluttering old man.

* * *

There had been something almost petulant in the gesture, for gesture it certainly had been. Eric Ward was left with a sense of shame and disgust at himself and as he thought back over the incident he questioned why he had done it. The conclusion he reached was that he had been infected by Amos Saxby's own theatricality: it had been as though both of them were playing a game.

Throughout the interview at the Old Vicarage there had been an element of role-playing. Sam Saxby had played little or no part in it — he had merely been there, a pale prop in the background. Amos Saxby had held the centre of the stage, playing the dominant patriarch, sprawled in his chair while his visitor stood, denying time or information and yet leaking pieces, comments, statements even as he refused an interview. And Eric had been drawn into the plot, displaying his own kind of controlled aggression, refusing to be overcome by the muscle of the old man's personality, demanding the information that the old man said he would not give, and yet released, in his own time.

The scene in the bedroom was all part of the same scenario. In practical terms it had been unnecessary but they had all taken part in the charade, tramping up the stairs to view the stricken old woman as she lay, fearful and anxious, in her bed, unable to move or speak. Amos Saxby could have been satisfied merely by telling Eric Ward of the stroke and the paralysis; instead, a private viewing had been arranged.

And Eric Ward had played his own part in it all, even down to the final, dramatic scene in the doorway of the Old Vicarage.

Now, as he stood on the bridge at Wylam, watching the house martins skimming and flashing above the river in the soft evening air, he wondered whether anything in that twenty minutes or so that he had spent in Amos Saxby's house had been real. Amos had been standing back all the while — and so had Eric Ward, curiously enough. It was not something he was proud of, though it convinced him of the chameleon nature of character, the donning of a new skin to match the surrounding emotional background. Even so, what left him puzzled was the motive behind Amos Saxby's attitude. For that matter, there was much about Amos Saxby that puzzled him. Three strapping sons; a lifetime farming and a planned retirement; a deliberate policy of looking after each of his sons, financially. And then the regard that presumably he had held for his wife could be ignored while he displayed her, paralysed in her bed; the deliberate evasion of a legal consequence that must, initially at least, have been precisely what he and Ellen Saxby had wanted.

He had been confident of his facts; and of the legal advice he had been given. He had been sure the option to purchase would be destroyed by the conveyance, and it had given him the confidence to play cat and mouse with Eric Ward, to the extent that maybe the whole play had been designed to push Eric into his own dramatic gesture — the service of the writ.

For Amos Saxby knew that he could win. And perhaps it was all about a public humiliation of his son Jack Saxby, a final and open display of his denial of Holton Hill Farm.

The man was soured towards his youngest son and he and Ellen had contrived to undo the plans they had had for him. Perhaps it had something to do with Sandra Saxby — she clearly had no love for the old man. And she would push

Jack Saxby into fighting the thing through to its inevitably bitter end. Even if, as Eric Ward still thought, they were bound to lose.

He had said so to Joseph Francis. But the senior partner had shaken his head. Perhaps they were looking at the matter in too clinical a light. Why not use a little imagination? A little legal reconstruction, perhaps?

'Let's consider the possibilities, dear boy. The writ is served: we played safe, claiming damages from Amos and Ellen Saxby for breach of the option to purchase. But we both know that'll not do Jack Saxby much good. Because if Amos Saxby has a legal adviser worth his salt he'll be told to take evasive action: he'll get rid of most of his assets, maybe by a conveyance to Samuel and Colin Saxby on a trust basis. There'd be nothing left for Jack Saxby to proceed against. So damages ... no point in such an action.'

Eric Ward had agreed with Joseph's view.

'But,' Joseph had continued, 'what if we ask the court to take a look at the *motives* in Amos and Ellen Saxby's minds? What then?'

And after a little while Eric had agreed, again.

The result now, was *Saxby v Saxby*, in the Crown Court.

* * *

Briefing Charlie Dawson had been a bit of a gamble. Joseph Francis had argued for a while: Dawson was a good, solid, dependable, middle-of-the-road criminal man, whose major experience lay in the police courts, and in a civil issue of this kind he might be out of his depth. Eric disagreed.

'Charlie Dawson is a methodical man and a good cross-examiner. He also possesses a subtlety which he's developed over the years in lulling offenders before going for the jugular. I've seen him do it so often — all right, the cases have been small beer, but the technique has been right. And I have a feeling he could work well here. Because the fact is, Amos Saxby sees himself above all this. He played with me out at the Old Vicarage; he's confident and bitter and *certain*. That makes him vulnerable because his certainty may, as you suggest, be misplaced.' When he caught Joseph Francis's self-satisfied smile, grudgingly Eric had nodded. 'All right, I agree, maybe I was wrong. I still think we've a long hill to climb, but I consider Charlie Dawson is the right man to lead us up it …'To try to make the charge stick: that Amos and Ellen Saxby were guilty of a conspiracy to defraud their client — Jack Saxby, of Holton Hill Farm.'

* * *

The courtroom was crowded from the first day because newspaper coverage had already made it into a local *cause célèbre*. After preliminary discussions and an inspection of the documents disclosed, Charlie Dawson had advised Eric that it would be as well to join Sam Saxby as a co-defendant; when Eric had doubted the wisdom of that step Charlie had pointed out that since it seemed Sam had been one of the witnesses to the conveyance there was the chance that he had been involved in the whole thing. And if he were not joined as defendant it was unlikely he would agree to give evidence against Amos and Ellen.

'Moreover,' Charlie advised, 'it will prevent Amos transferring assets to Sam to avoid judgment if the case goes against him.'

Eric Ward agreed and Amos, Ellen and Sam Saxby were joined as co-defendants to the conspiracy claim.

Charlie Dawson was obviously enjoying the brief he had been given and during the first day of the hearing he took full advantage of the appearance of Sam Saxby, drawing out the fact that Sam had been a signatory to the conveyance and laying ironic doubt upon Sam's claim that he knew nothing of the motivation that had inspired Amos and Ellen Saxby to try to evade the option to purchase.

'But didn't it seem odd to you, Mr Saxby, that your father and mother wished to take this step?'

'It was my mother's property to do with as she wished, in freehold terms.'

'But I am right in saying that Amos Saxby had conveyed Eastgate Farm — after a proving tenancy — to you, and Brookfield Farm to your brother Colin?'

'That is correct.'

'In both cases, to set you up in life?'

'I suppose so.'

'Then why the different attitude towards Jack Saxby and Holton Hill Farm?'

'That's not for me to say. It was their decision.'

'Which you did not question?'

'It was not my place to question.'

'You weren't even *curious?*'

'It was my father's decision.'

Charlie Dawson paused, eyed Sam Saxby carefully for a long-drawn-out moment. 'Your *father's* decision?'

'My *parents'* decision,' Sam Saxby corrected himself.

'It wasn't Ellen Saxby's idea?'

'They were in agreement.'

Charlie Dawson paused again. 'Would you describe your father as a forceful man ... a dominant personality?'

There was a short silence.

'Well?' Charlie Dawson prompted.

'He, he, has a strong personality.'

'And he pressed this matter upon your mother?'

'I didn't say that.'

At the defendants' table Amos Saxby stirred restlessly and at the end of the day's proceedings he swept out of the courtroom, glaring at Eric Ward as he did so. But it was on the third day of the hearing that Charlie Dawson really came into his own and the briefing, insisted upon by Eric Ward, bore fruit.

The witness called was Mr Stanley Cranby, solicitor, of the firm of Cranby and Grafton. He was a small, rotund man in standard uniform: blue, pin-striped suit, white shirt and blue collar. His eyes were small and button-black, his mouth loose and nervous; small tufts of sandy hair above his ears tended to emphasize the naked baldness of his head, shining and glistening as he took his place in the witness-box. Charlie Dawson moved up to him like a gentle cobra.

'Mr Cranby ... of Cranby and Grafton. That's a Berwick firm, I understand.'

'That is so.'

'You have *your* office in Berwick?'

'I do.'

'Have you had previous dealings with the Saxby family?'

Mr Cranby moistened his lips. 'I have done some work for Mr Sam Saxby in the past, in relation to certain landholdings in Northumberland.'

'Well, that was understandable ... but were you not ... ah ... surprised to be called in for *this* conveyance?'

'Surprised? No. It was a normal conveyance. It was within my line of business.'

'But,' Charlie suggested softly, 'Berwick is rather a long way from Morpeth.'

Mr Cranby made no reply but raised a disdainful eyebrow.

'There are other firms in Morpeth, and between Morpeth and Berwick aren't there?' Charlie asked.

'Of course.'

'Then why you?'

'I assume,' Cranby said with dignity, 'because I was recommended by Mr Sam Saxby, who was satisfied by the way I had handled his other affairs.'

'Was Amos Saxby satisfied in this matter?'

'I believe so.'

'So what did you do for him?'

Mr Cranby blinked. 'I beg your pardon?'

'Let's go through the whole transaction, step by step, so you can explain why Amos and Ellen Saxby used your firm. Let's see what special services you were able to provide.'

'Nothing special—'

'How were you first retained?'

Mr Cranby considered for a moment. 'A phone call, from Mr Sam Saxby.'

'*Sam* Saxby. I see.'

'He said his father wished to retain me in a conveyancing matter.'

'Hmmm. You didn't think it odd you should receive this work, rather than the family solicitors, Francis, Shaw and Elder?' Charlie Dawson asked.

'That was a decision for Mr Amos Saxby.'

'I see. Fine. So … tell us what happened. How did you get your instructions?'

Mr Cranby licked his lips. 'As a result of the telephone conversation I drove down to Morpeth.'

'*You* drove *down?* Well, well! When was that?'

'The next day.'

'The very next day,' Charlie said in mock wonderment. 'It must have been an important matter.'

'I was told so.'

'What happened then?'

'I met Mr Sam Saxby at the Old Vicarage and he introduced me to his mother and father.'

'Had you met them before?'

'No.'

'How did they instruct you?'

'Mr Amos Saxby explained that for purposes of agricultural investment and tax avoidance he wished to arrange for a conveyance of Holton Hill Farm, presently held under a tenancy agreement by Mr Jack Saxby. The conveyance was to be to Mr Amos Saxby; the sale was to be by Mrs Ellen Saxby.'

'I see. So you drove fifty miles or so to take instructions on a family conveyance from wife to husband.' Charlie Dawson paused for effect. 'And immediately. Hmmm. What happened then?'

'Mrs Ellen Saxby gave me authority to collect the title deeds from the bank in Morpeth, where they were deposited.'

'What date did this take place?'

'The meeting at the Old Vicarage was March 15th.'

'When did you collect the deeds?'

'The same day.'

'You conducted a search at the Registry, I suppose? I mean, that would be normal practice.'

'I did,' Cranby said earnestly.

'Did you then complete the conveyance?'

'Yes.'

'Where?'

Cranby appeared nonplussed for a moment. 'I don't understand.' He shook his bald head. 'There were further enquiries ...'

'Did you take the deeds back to Berwick?'

'Well, no. I ... I made use of certain facilities at Morpeth to complete the paperwork.'

Charlie Dawson inspected an affidavit in his left hand. 'Ah ... those facilities were granted you by the legal firm of Bragg and Clees, of Morpeth?'

'That's right. We have had dealings with them from time to time and ...' Cranby's voice died away as Charlie Dawson stared at him.

'And on what date did you work at the Morpeth office, Mr Cranby?'

'March 16th.'

'And on what date was the conveyance completed?'

Cranby looked uneasy and shifted in his seat. 'March 17th.'

His Honour Judge Semple, Q.C. twisted his head to stare in disbelief at the sweating solicitor. He raised a hand, stopping Charlie Dawson as he prepared to ask another question.

'Did you say March 17th, Mr Cranby?'

'Yes, your Honour.'

'The conveyance was completed in *three days flat?*'

Cranby nodded nervously. 'Yes, your Honour.'

Judge Semple raised his eyebrows in amazement. 'I can only quote Mr Winston Churchill, in admiration: never in the history of conveyancing ...'

A ripple of laughter ran around the courtroom. Eric Ward looked at Amos Saxby. The old man was glaring at Cranby as though he could cheerfully have throttled him; his lean hands were clenched on the table in front of him, knuckles knotted whitely.

'So you borrowed office space ... and a secretary's services ... and you completed the conveyance. You took it back to the Old Vicarage?'

'Yes.'

'Completion took place there, on the 17th?'

'Yes.'

'And in executing the conveyance, presumably the price was paid, and handled by you, the responsible solicitor. A cheque?'

'Yes.'

'A cheque drawn on Mr Amos Saxby's account ...' Charlie Dawson shuffled the papers on his desk, selected a bank statement. 'I obtained this under discovery of documents. The cheque in question is this one?'

Cranby looked at the statement. 'Yes. For £500.'

'Do you notice anything about the account, Mr Cranby?'

Cranby stared, hesitated, glanced towards Amos Saxby and moistened his lips again. 'It ... the account seems to have been overdrawn on the 17th of March.'

There was a short silence. Judge Semple leaned forward.

'Mr Dawson, it is getting rather late in the day. Do you wish very much more time with this witness?'

'I have only a few more points to make, your Honour.'

Judge Semple nodded, satisfied. He always liked to be back in good time for his evening glass of wine.

'What would Holton Hill Farm be worth at present prices, Mr Cranby?'

'I wouldn't know. And the price was of no relevance—'

'Forty thousand pounds? More?'

Cranby shrugged. 'I suppose so. But—'

'And the price paid was *five hundred pounds.*'

'Yes, but—'

'When you made your search of the Register, did it disclose anything?'

'No.'

'An option to purchase, charged as an estate contract against Holton Hill Farm?'

'No. Nothing. No encumbrances.'

'Did you know of the existence of such an, unregistered, charge?'

'I did not.'

'Tell me this, then, Mr Cranby. If you *had* known of the existence of such a charge, unregistered though it was, would you have undertaken the conveyance?'

Cranby hesitated, flashed a quick, nervous look towards Amos Saxby. 'No, I would not.'

'Why?'

'Ethically—'

'Do you now understand why you were asked to undertake this conveyance, Mr Cranby?'

'I—'

'Do you understand why it was necessary to use a firm other than the family firm, to defeat the unregistered option to purchase; do you understand why the great haste was necessary, when any day that option could be registered, if Jack Saxby had got wind of what was going on; do you understand that the £500 was a merely nominal sum, one that was even drawn on an overdue account because in the indecent haste to get the transaction completed there had been no check on the state of that account? You're a lawyer, Mr Cranby; you're experienced in the ways of the world. Give me your professional opinion; explain to me what you think of this whole shady transaction! It was all a plot, wasn't it, Mr Cranby? You were the dupe of Amos and Ellen Saxby: they used you because they couldn't use their own solicitor; they pushed you into the quickest conveyance on record, not giving you time to even think. They used an overdrawn bank account; they hid from you the existence of the estate contract; and it was a plot, a conspiracy to defeat the interest of my client Jack Saxby! Isn't that the way it was, Mr Cranby? Don't you see it in that light?'

'I ...' Cranby was flustered.

Judge Semple intervened. 'Mr Dawson, a little control, please. You are asking the witness to make suppositions, draw inferences which are hardly his to draw. The court, on the other hand ...'

'Thank you, your Honour. I was carried away,' Charlie Dawson said cheerfully. 'I have no further questions of this witness. Just a piece of advice for Mr Cranby.' He smiled expansively. 'Don't do this kind of thing again, Mr Cranby: a hasty lawyer is a careless lawyer. You have to certify the value of land conveyed don't you, for tax and stamp duty purposes?'

'Of course.'

Charlie Dawson grinned. 'You'd better check your certification. Amos Saxby had you spinning so fast you even got that wrong. You certified its value as £5,000. It should have been eight times that amount. He really did have you going, didn't he, Mr Cranby? But never mind. We'll find out why, tomorrow.' Charlie Dawson glanced around the courtroom. 'When, Mr Amos Saxby takes the stand, tomorrow, then we'll find out why.'

* * *

In the event, Charlie Dawson was wrong.

The next morning they were all there in the courtroom. Seated just behind Eric Ward was Jack Saxby and his wife Sandra. A few yards away were the legal representatives of Amos and Ellen Saxby, and behind them sat Sam Saxby and his brother Colin. To Eric it was a classical situation and one of which he had warned Jack Saxby at the beginning: family rifts were the worst and would leave a legacy of bitterness, a wound that might never heal.

Amos Saxby was in the witness-box. His eyes seemed to be more piercing in their glance than ever but the doubts raised by Cranby's evidence had evidently taken their toll because there were blue marks of tiredness, bruises of fatigue beneath his eyes. His face seemed gaunter, the lined skin now deeply furrowed around the mouth, and though his bristly grey hair still stood up stiffly and defiantly, there was something new in his bearing, something different in the manner in which he stared at Eric Ward's client. It was a glare of pure malevolence.

Charlie Dawson was asking him a question but Amos Saxby made no reply. The question was repeated, and after a short silence Judge Semple leaned forward and said, 'Mr Saxby, do you intend answering the question? If you do not—'

He was not given the chance to complete the remark. Amos Saxby suddenly threw back his head and raised one stiff, quivering arm. The menace in his pointing finger was directed towards the paling Jack Saxby.

'I was alone at the Old Vicarage last night,' the old man thundered. 'I was alone, there with none of my sons near me. And at three o'clock this morning the woman I was nursing — your mother — died! You were responsible for her death and I'm letting it be known here, now, in public! You killed her with your greed and your anger and I tell you, I swear to you before all these people, Holton Hill Farm is mine, and you'll never get your hands on it.' His fingers closed into a fist and he stabbed at the air in a fierce, theatrical gesture. 'You'll never get it! I'll see you dead, and burning in hell before I ever let you get your hands on that farm!'

CHAPTER 3

There were occasions when the pilocarpine did not work as effectively as it should. Eric was never sure why it happened; it was possibly the result of his not noting the danger signals soon enough and applying the drug too late. On such occasions he suffered for his lack of care, when the scratching began against the nerve ends behind his eyeballs and he was forced to retreat to the washroom and get over the shuddering and the excruciating pain in private .

He had such an attack two weeks after the funeral of Mrs Saxby. He was in court when he felt the attack coming on; the room was crowded, the judge summing up, but he could not wait. He rose, struggled out through the press, and was almost staggering when he finally made it to the cloakroom.

There he waited, miserable, scared, and in considerable pain. It was coming, he knew it was coming: he had put off the decision to go ahead with the operation but soon it would be forced upon him merely by the resurgence of such an attack as this. He was losing his courage — it was a different kind of courage that he had needed to face a thug on a drunken Saturday night with a broken bottle in his hand. That had been a police matter, part of the job, you just went in and did it. But this was so *personal*, and so terrifying in the knowledge that the pain was there all the time, just waiting to reach out, waiting to score with its needles of agony against his eyes.

He made his way back to the office in a state of desperation. If the operation were to be unsuccessful it would mean the end of his new career, a career he had only just started. Francis, Shaw and Elder would hardly have room for a blind solicitor.

He sat in his room and stared at the telephone. There was no point in waiting any longer. He might just as well get the whole thing over. He reached out to pick up the phone, to call Mr Callaghan for an appointment.

The phone jangled before he touched it. It was Philippa.

'Mr Ward, there's a gentleman in reception who's asking if you're free to see him for a few minutes. He doesn't have an appointment, and if you're busy I can easily put him off. But you're back early from court so I thought that—'

'Did he give his name?'

'It's a Mr Samuel Saxby.'

'*Sam* Saxby?' Eric Ward paused, then ran his hand lightly over his swollen eyes. 'All right, I'll see him. Send him up in a few minutes, will you?'

He rose, went to the washroom and bathed his eyes and forehead; he looked at his hands. They had stopped shaking now and he was more in control of himself. Work, concentration on legal matters, it could be a palliative, he thought.

He went back to his room. A few minutes later Philippa introduced Sam Saxby.

Amos Saxby's eldest son wore a black armband in memory of his mother. His face was grim. There was much of the old man in him, Eric considered: the same jut of the jaw, the same build. But in some indefinable way he lacked Amos Saxby's strength and determination; he was not possessed of the same kind of drive. It was likely he would have the same kind of ambitions as the old man, but he would seek to achieve them in different, subtler ways.

For a farmer, his hands were soft.

'Well, Mr Saxby, what can I do for you?'

'Amos doesn't know I'm here.'

Eric nodded, but made no comment. 'This whole thing's gone too far,' Sam Saxby said peevishly. 'But the old man won't see sense. I've tried to talk to him, but ... What's likely to happen now, Mr Ward?'

Eric shrugged. 'The hearing was adjourned after your father's outburst; Judge Semple, quite rightly, wasn't prepared to go on with the hearing in the surrounding circumstances. But the case will be rescheduled in due course — largely dependent upon the instructions I get from my client.'

Sam Saxby frowned. 'I've had a word with Jack, too. He's as stubborn as Amos.'

'He feels he has cause for complaint,' Eric said quietly.

Sam Saxby stared at him. 'Amos will never give in. He meant what he said in the courtroom.'

There was a tiny throbbing at the back of Eric Ward's eyes. 'Your father,' he replied irritably, 'is somewhat given to extravagant gestures.'

Sam Saxby paused, then sat down. With Eric's permission he lit a cigarette and drew on it, suddenly nervous. 'This conspiracy to defraud claim ... whose idea was it?'

'The facts drawn out so far would seem to support the claim. It makes no difference who thought of it.'

'It'll be Jack's wife who's pushing it. She hates Amos; always has. But this conspiracy thing ... it wasn't like that, I assure you. I had no idea ... I just witnessed the conveyance.'

'And introduced your father to Mr Cranby.'

Sam Saxby's eyes did not meet his. 'Do you think Jack would compromise?'

'In what way?'

'Settle for damages, or something.'

'You'd have to discuss that with him personally — or instruct your solicitor to call on me. I really can't discuss it with you like this.'

'No. Suppose not. But it would be sensible, wouldn't it? This case is tearing the family apart.'

'I would have thought the wounds were there before the case came on,' Eric suggested. 'Why on earth did your father and mother reach that decision, to sell the farm to Amos?'

Sam Saxby drew on his cigarette. He narrowed his eyes against the smoke and did not meet Eric Ward's questioning glance. He shook his head. 'Amos said it was a matter of tax avoidance.'

'And you believed that?'

'I didn't know what to believe. I tell you, I was just involved as a signatory. I should never have been joined as a co-defendant in this conspiracy charge. I didn't plot. And if the case goes against me, it's I'm the one now who's going to have to carry the can, isn't it? Amos, he's all right, he's got the Old Vicarage and a bit salted away and he won't need much anyway, especially now that Mother's gone. But me, everything I've got of any consequence is tied up in Eastgate Farm. I bought another property a few years ago in Northumberland — that was when I first used Cranby — but it was a disaster, it just didn't pay, and the manager I put in was next to useless. I lost money on that deal, and I'm pretty strapped right now as far as ready cash is concerned.'

'You also had the expense of litigation over Eastgate Farm, didn't you?'

For a moment Sam Saxby looked startled. 'The wayleave thing, you mean? Well, it wasn't a big deal. Mr Francis sorted it out.' A shadow passed over his eyes momentarily and in a nervous gesture he stubbed out his half-smoked cigarette. 'No, it didn't cost much and was quickly dealt with. But right now, if Jack was awarded damages against me, I don't know how I'd scrape it together, the way things are.'

'Your father wouldn't help you?'

Sam Saxby snorted derisively. 'You don't know Amos. He wouldn't lift a finger. He's a devotee of Samuel Smiles self-help and all that sort of thing. Oh, all right, he's set me up, and Colin too, and to the outsider that looks pretty good, the generous, caring father. But there's another way of looking at it too, you know. It's a way of getting rid of your responsibilities. When Amos sold Eastgate Farm to me, after making me work it for a few years, he effectively washed his hands, said there's one out of the way, and that was that. If I ever went back to the old man for help he'd laugh in my face. No, he wouldn't lift a finger.'

'Does he have the same attitude towards your brother Colin?' Eric asked.

''It was a bit more complicated there.' Sam Saxby seemed about to say more but decided against it and Eric was left with the impression that relationships within the Saxby family were somewhat uneasy; the undercurrents were strong. 'No,' Sam Saxby continued, 'it's the same with Colin. He was given the tenancy of Brookfield Farm when he came out of the Army and then it was made over to him for a nominal price thereafter. The old man played fair from there on. But if Colin was in trouble now, Amos wouldn't lift a finger. He shuffled off his parental dues by selling Colin Brookfield: Colin will now have to sink or swim.'

'But at least both you and your brother Colin have been given a sound base to start from,' Eric Ward murmured. 'Why hasn't Amos done it for Jack?'

'I—' Sam Saxby hesitated, glanced around the room as though seeking support. 'I don't know. Jack's always been ... different from me and Colin, somehow. There was a time when I thought he was Amos's favourite ... youngest son and all that. But there's a funny streak in Jack. He's a good farmer, but there's more of Mother in him than Amos. He never did have the drive that Amos wanted to see ... and maybe that's why Amos changed his mind over the farm. Maybe that's what it was.'

'But you don't believe that.'

Sam Saxby looked at Ward sharply. 'No, I suppose not. It is a bit lame, isn't it? You ... you'll have met Jack's wife?'

'Yes.'

Sam Saxby grimaced. 'Maybe it was on account of her.'

Eric Ward hesitated. 'She doesn't get on with Amos?' He leaned forward in his chair. 'Was she the cause of the estrangement?'

'These are family matters, Mr Ward.'

'You're not obliged to discuss them,' Ward conceded. 'I'm sorry, I shouldn't pry, but I thought it might be helpful, to get the complete picture.'

'That's all right. Well ... I suppose it doesn't make much difference, anyway, because the whole relationship's pretty obvious in any case.' Saxby's eyes dwelled on Eric for several seconds, weighing things up. 'What conclusions have you drawn from Amos's treatment of my brother Colin?'

Eric scratched his chin thoughtfully. 'I'm slightly surprised by Amos's forbearance, I suppose.'

'In what way?'

'Well, from what I've seen of Amos Saxby he wouldn't have taken kindly to Colin giving up farming, not once, but twice. First, when he went off to the Army; second, when he came back, was given Brookfield Farm, and then sold it to go into other forms of business. Amos seems to have been almost ... indulgent, for him.'

Sam Saxby smiled, but his eyes remained cool. 'That was because it was a bit more complicated than that. Amos felt he owed Colin something; there was a bit of the prodigal's return, too, when Colin came back from the Army. Amos felt good, at the thought Colin was seeing sense at last.'

'What happened, then?'

'It was all over Sandra ... Sandra King as she was called then.'

'Sandra ... and Colin?'

Sam Saxby nodded. 'Sandra was the daughter of one of the labourers at Eastgate Farm. There was a bit of trouble, some petty theft or something, and King got turned out of the tied cottage, went to live in Chollerford. King was pretty bitter about it. But then all hell broke loose, because Colin went to see the old man. He wanted to marry Sandra.'

'I see.'

Sam Saxby grinned viciously. 'Amos didn't see at all. He wasn't having his son marrying the daughter of a thieving farm labourer. There was a shouting match. Amos won, but only in part. He broke Colin, but Colin couldn't stay around. He shoved off, joined the Army, got a commission, stayed out of the way for a few years, and when he came back—'

'It was to find Sandra had married his brother.' Eric Ward shook his head. 'Amos can't have enjoyed that too much.'

'I told you: Jack was always a bit different from me and Colin. To tell the truth, I'd have buckled under the old man too, like Colin. Jack didn't. He stood up to him. He might lack the drive that Amos always had, the ambition to get a good farm going, but he can be stubborn, can Jack. And I thought at the time maybe Amos respected him for sticking out. Anyway, Jack married Sandra and that was that. But maybe I was wrong, with hindsight; maybe Amos never did forgive Jack for marrying her. And he never intended that Jack should get set up the way me and Colin were. It's the only reason why I can think ...'

'Sandra Saxby clearly dislikes Amos,' Eric ventured.

'Like poison.' Sam Saxby replied. 'Never made any secret of it. But there it is, Mr Ward. The family skeletons are rattling out. And now the bloodletting is to be done in open court. But I can't afford that. I've too much tied up in Eastgate.'

'I'm sorry about that, but I don't see how I can help,' Eric said.

'You could persuade Jack to back off ... drop the case against Amos, and me.'

'Why should I do that, Mr Saxby?'

'Because Amos will never give in. You heard him in court. And damn it, I was never involved in any bloody conspiracy over this thing!'

Eric Ward hesitated. He eyed Sam Saxby quietly for a little while and then decided to explain the situation to him. There seemed little reason to make the man continue to labour under the anxiety of a threatened resumption of the court hearing. 'Things might now have changed, Mr Saxby.'

'How do you mean?'

'The death of your mother will have made a certain difference, tactically speaking.'

'I don't understand.'

'You'll be aware that your mother made a will. It was prepared in this office. The only beneficiary is your father Amos: she left all property she might own at her death to him.'

'Yes, I know that — not that she had a great deal to leave as it happened, once Holton Hill Farm was transferred to the old man.'

Eric nodded. 'That's the point, really. You see, I've advised your brother Jack that we *could* proceed with the conspiracy issue, but in the circumstances it might be less unpleasant, for all concerned, if we were to hold that matter in abeyance.'

'You mean drop the whole thing?'

'I didn't say that. No, take proceedings against someone other than members of the family itself.'

Sam Saxby frowned. 'You've lost me.'

'The nominated executors of your mother's will are the National Bank. It is their responsibility to distribute the estate. I have spoken to your brother Jack and pointed out that it might be better, to avoid the running sore of a family battle, to take proceedings against the bank. In other words, I've advised him to proceed in court, using the bank as defendants, asking for a declaration that the option to purchase Holton Hill Farm is binding upon her estate; calling for specific performance of that contract; and damages in lieu of specific performance.' Eric paused. 'Only then would we pursue the fourth count in the statement of claim — if we need to, having failed under the other heads damages for conspiracy. I don't think it will need to come to that, Mr Saxby.'

But to Eric's surprise, he was left with a feeling that Sam Saxby was not entirely satisfied with the result.

* * *

And yet, there was more than Sam Saxby's blankness of expression to go on, in addition, there had been something odd about the whole interview. Sam Saxby had certainly been worried and concerned about his likely liability in a conspiracy suit, but his talk with Eric Ward had not been a straightforward one. There had been something tentative about it, as though he had been trying out some ideas, bouncing a metal ball against a wall, seeking responses and reactions.

Amos Saxby was a man who throve on theatricality: Eric could just imagine the thundering scene that must have occurred when Colin Saxby told Amos he wanted to marry Sandra King.

But Sam Saxby was a different proposition: the eldest son had a reticence, a hidden undercurrent that was controlled and directed. In some way, while his feelings had been exposed in Eric's office, he had yet contrived to hold something back. Something, Eric suspected, of significance. But then he thrust further thoughts of Sam Saxby from his mind as he received another phone call.

It was Anne Morcomb.

'Are you going tonight?'

'Where?'

She laughed; it had a warm, friendly sound. 'Grey's Restaurant, of course.'

'What's on there?'

'Really ... *men!* And you in particular, Eric Ward! Have you looked in your mail recently?'

'Of course. But I—'

'And didn't you see an invitation from Stoneleigh Enterprises among all the other important mail?'

He had; he had consigned it to the wastepaper-basket. 'I decided not to go — didn't think it was my kind of ... ah ... scene.'

'You mean you turned it down, after I had wangled you a special invitation? I tell you, my friend, I had to work at it. Antony Stoneleigh wasn't all that keen. But I persuaded him.'

'Why?' Eric asked bluntly.

'Because I thought your charm, your panache, your gay laugh, your presence would light up the room! Really, Eric, asking me a question like that! Can't it just be that I looked forward to your company on this occasion? Would you settle for that?'

'I would have thought the Honourable Antony would have been dancing attendance,' Eric said.

There was a short pause. He thought he detected a smile in her voice when she replied. 'I think he *wanted* to, but was rather torn by . . . other possibilities being available. And besides ...'

'Yes?'

'I really have a particular reason for wanting to go. And with you.'

'Should I feel flattered?'

'If you like. Will you go ... and escort me?'

'If you tell me the particular reason.'

'Right,' she said briskly. 'That's settled then.'

'And the reason?'

'I'll tell you later.'

And with that Eric Ward had to be satisfied.

* * *

During the hours that followed he found himself thinking a good deal about Anne Morcomb.

The events that had thrown them together before her father's death had, he knew, left her with the feeling that she was falling in love with him. It was a situation he had deliberately walked away from, for several reasons. It was pretty clear now that she had got over what was little more than a schoolgirl crush and could treat him in a sensible, balanced, friendly manner; on the other hand, he was forced to admit to himself that if he spent too much time in her company the rejecting role he had assumed two years ago would be more difficult to maintain. For he was attracted to her, even though he knew nothing could come of it.

She had asked him to call for her at eight. She had given him the address of a flat in Montague Court: though she still lived at Sedleigh Hall and administered the Morcomb estates from there. She had found it necessary to obtain a base in Newcastle as it meant she did not have to face the long drive out into Northumberland if she was in town late, and it was also useful for business reasons from time to time.

Eric left the office at five and spent an hour or so working at some files before he took a shower and changed, then drove back into Newcastle to meet her. He parked outside the impressive block of flats, took the lift up to the top floor and she met him in a thickly carpeted hallway with a smile, an apology and an explanation that she was almost ready and would he like to pour himself a drink? He settled for a soft drink and then stood at the tall window, looking out over the city and the light mist that was rising along the Tyne. In the distance he could see the lights twinkling on; along to Durham hills, and across to the right, car headlights along the road past Wylam, flashing and dipping along the highway in the darkening evening.

'I sometimes sit here after dark, and just watch.'

The dress she wore was simple, black and devastating. Above the low neckline her skin seemed to glow; he was aware of the way the dress moulded her figure but his own glance was riveted by hers. There was something mocking in her eyes, the hint of a challenge that he did not understand … or want to understand. He turned away, refusing to accept it, and said, 'Yes, it's quite a view from up here.'

She chuckled softly and he felt his neck getting red. Stiffly, he said, 'It's certainly a far cry from my humble cottage at Wylam.'

'I will admit this place is rather more than comfortable. But there are advantages too, living in a small village like Wylam.'

He thought of the martins along the river bank, the phosphorescent tracks of rising fish in the early summer evenings, and he nodded, looked back at her. She was still staring at him but the mockery had gone; there was a softer message in her eyes now.

'Well, if you're ready, we'd better make a move,' he said, injecting a briskness into his tone to break the moment. He finished his soft drink but she had turned away and was pouring herself a gin and tonic. She smiled at him, sat down, and after a moment he sat down too, on an easy chair facing her.

'I don't like being first arrival at a party,' she said. 'Besides, it's rather interesting seeing you here, the fly in the spider's web.'

'Is that how you see yourself?'

'Why not? Poor little rich girl and all that sort of thing.'

He had a suspicion that the conversation might head in a direction he did not want, and he had not yet sufficiently recovered his equilibrium to develop it into light banter.

'I didn't really read the invitation,' he said hurriedly, 'So I'm not particularly clear what we're going to. What's it all about?'

'Sir John Freshfield.'

'The junior Minister?'

'And merchant banker,' Anne said. 'The Honourable Antony has finally succeeded in getting him to come along. They'll have had a business session this afternoon — I believe Tony took him down to Seaham to discuss the developments — and this evening is a sort of softener, I suppose, a way of ... entertaining Sir John before he goes back to London in the morning.'

Eric eyed her warily. There was an odd look in her eye, and an enforced primness about her smile that made him uneasy. 'I ... I suppose Stoneleigh will be hoping for some kind of support from Freshfield's bank.'

'That'll be the general idea.'

'There's nothing about financial support in the papers I've seen from Stoneleigh, but I suppose ...'

'He's got to get money for development purposes, and get political support for an area plan. I think he's trying to kill several birds with one stone — and Sir John has important local political connections as well. Oh, if *I* know Tony, he'll have all sorts of expectations of the wheeler-dealer kind this evening.'

'And you do know him pretty well, don't you?'

'Well enough,' Anne replied, and eyed him mockingly over the rim of her glass.

Conversation lapsed for a little while. Eric Ward stared out across the darkening city, aware that Anne was still watching him. At last she said, 'I heard about the noise and thunder in court the other day.'

'Amos Saxby?' Eric shrugged. 'He likes an audience.'

'His wife had just *died,*' Anne reproved him.

'Well, yes, maybe my comment sounded a bit unfeeling. Even so, Amos Saxby ... there would have been other ways to show his feelings. You see, it looks as though none of his sons knew she'd died that morning. All three were in court. They got the message like the rest of the courtroom — by way of Amos's towering threat. Hardly the way to behave to your children, I would have thought. But Amos, well, that's the way he chose to make the unhappy announcement.'

'You're saying he was *using* the situation?'

'Milking it for all it was worth.'

'That's ... horrible.'

'I agree. But the family ...' Eric hesitated. 'It's not the closest-knit group I've seen. It's riven with tension, and there are curious discrepancies in the way they seem to behave and look at each other. I mean, on the face of it, old

Amos was a good father, following a deliberate supportive policy towards the future of his sons. Setting up Sam, then Colin ... But Jack is suddenly left out in the cold, and I get the feeling the old man doesn't care too much for his other two sons either.'

'He couldn't,' Anne murmured. 'Not if he treats them in that way, letting them know in the courtroom that their mother had just died. It's ... unfeeling.'

'Maybe he thinks they don't deserve better treatment. But how one reconciles that with his earlier attitudes ... It's as though something cataclysmic happened recently ...'

'That's a long word for a solicitor.'

'Cataclysms do occur, even in lawyer's lives.'

'I know.' She was silent for a little while, staring at him. 'How are you, Eric?'

'Fit, strong, clear-eyed as ever,' he bantered. 'As long as I stay off the kind of stuff you're drinking. Ah ... *that's* why you wanted me to squire you this evening. You wanted to be sure there'd be a sober driver to bring you back home!'

'Something like that,' she said, and smiled.

'Do I get no more information?'

'Not at present. Right, shall we go?'

* * *

The Honourable Antony Stoneleigh had prepared the ground well. He had taken over a large room at Grey's and the waiter at the damasked table in the corner was serving champagne to each arrival before they moved on down the room to meet Stoneleigh and the guest of honour. The room was crowded, and almost everyone of importance seemed to be there — including the Lord Lieutenant, the Chief Constables of the two northern forces, a scattering of legal and masonic notables, including Joseph Francis, a selection of leading lights from the business community, senior civil servants from Washington and Darlington, and a boisterous group from the Northumberland Hunt. At the far end of the room a splendid buffet supper had been laid out and, if the music that gently edged itself into the consciousness was piped, at least it had the advantage of discreet quality.

Which was something that could not be said about Sir John Freshfield. Eric had never met him, though he had seen him occasionally on television. He had not liked what he had seen, but a view of the actual flesh did nothing to alleviate the unfavourable screen impression. Freshfield was a larger than life figure, with strong handsome features marred by a network of red, destroyed veins in his nose; his voice was an impressive, booming baritone but he used it overmuch, overlaying, smothering conversation with it, relegating other people's views and comments to a trampled, drowned submission. He laughed too much and too easily, greeted people with too much pleasure, enjoyed company and conversation and life too much. For his eyes were small and cold and they reflected the man within. He was a political animal in the business of selling himself; that major preoccupation would forestall all the other realities in his world and make them count for nothing. His aim would be the subordination of everything to the wants and needs of Sir John Freshfield.

He was a successful man.

One of the young Hunt bloods had already dragged Anne away from Eric and he was not distressed about it; he had no desire to keep her exclusively at his side, and he felt he could enjoy the opportunity to watch and listen more if he were alone. So he drifted, stopping for a brief conversation with Joseph Francis, meeting a few new faces and obtaining introductions, talking to old friends, and holding a short conversation with the Chief Constable of the Northumbria Force. The noise levels began to rise in direct ratio to the consumption of alcohol and Eric moved out after a while, seeking fresh air, aware that if he stayed too long in the thickening atmosphere, the heat and the pressure and the noise would have its effect upon him, and Anne Morcomb might find herself without an escort. And she had not yet told him why she had particularly wanted Eric Ward to bring her to the party.

The air outside was fresh and cool. Eric stood chatting for a few minutes to the grey-toppered doorman until a taxi drew up and the man hurried forward to greet its occupant.

It was Paul Francis.

He paid off the taxi-driver, turned and saw Eric. 'Hello — getting some fresh air? What's it like in the bear garden?'

'Just as you say. Noisy and hot.'

Paul Francis grinned, looked around him and sniffed at the air. 'Well, you'd never be able to convince a Londoner that it is possible to have parties outside in the balmy Northumberland evenings. Still, must do my duty and all that ...' He paused, as he was about to walk past Eric. 'Bit of noise in your court the other day, hey?'

'That's one way of putting it,' Eric agreed.

'What's to be the next step?'

'I've spoken to Jack Saxby. We'll be issuing another writ-against the executors now.'

'The bank?' Paul Francis nodded. 'Well, that should be interesting. They'll fight. Bloody banks always do. Ah, well—'

'Paul?'

The barrister stopped as he was walking past Eric. He turned his head; his narrow features seemed suddenly to hold a hint of wariness. 'Yes?'

'That option to purchase ... drawn up for Ellen Saxby in favour of her son Jack. It *was* you, wasn't it? You drew it up.'

Paul Francis stared at him, his eyes blank in the glare of the entrance lights. He shrugged. 'I ... I really can't remember. You'll forgive me, now, Eric. I'd better get inside.'

But it had been Paul Francis. Eric felt sure of it. For it made sense of Joseph Francis's initial reactions. It was not merely the possibility of a negligence suit against Francis, Shaw and Elder — it was the exposure of Paul Francis as an incompetent, at a time when he was beginning to make strides at the Bar. Joseph Francis had wanted to protect his only son: he knew that Paul had drawn up the option and had failed to register it. It was a fact he did not want to become public knowledge.

And, Eric thought, it might now never become public knowledge, for it could become submerged under the overall picture, the battle for Holton Hill Farm. For battle there would certainly be. Amos Saxby had already fired the opening shot and had, indeed, shown himself so fully committed to retention of the farm that he would pull out all the stops, do anything to hang on to the land. He had already used his wife's death to dramatize his stand: he had thrown down the gauntlet.

Eric wondered what else the vindictive old man might now dredge up to frustrate the son he hated.

* * *

After half an hour or so Eric wandered back into the restaurant. Groups were now moving along the lines of the tables, selecting from the buffet and the range of wines available. Eric was not hungry, so stayed, soft drink in hand, near the wall, watching the ebb and flow of conversation pieces, the drifters, the bores, the drunk, the noisy. He caught a glimpse of Colin Saxby paying heavy court to a tall, honey-haired woman with an obvious figure and even more obvious eyes. He seemed to be having a degree of success, but when Antony Stoneleigh passed, and spoke briefly to the girl, there was something in the way in which she lit up as he spoke that made Eric guess Colin Saxby would yet find the running competitive. Particularly if he continued to drink as heavily as he clearly had been doing, for his face had reddened, his voice had coarsened as the champagne and wine took its effect.

'Sprats and mackerel,' said the voice at Eric's elbow. 'Sprats and mackerel. Pretty hopeless exercise. It never really works. At least, not with a man like Sir John.' The speaker was small, lean, grey-suited, with an aquiline nose, cynical eyes and a bored, dissatisfied mouth. Like Eric, he was holding a soft drink in his hand, and he clearly saw other points of comparison. He looked Eric up and down and smiled thinly. 'Accountant? Stocks? Lawyer?'

'I'm a solicitor,' Eric Ward admitted.

'My name's Cranston. Professional watcher, you might say. And I advise on what I see.'

'You work with Sir John Freshfield?'

'You might say that. Though he won't need me to tell him about this kind of rubbish.'

Eric looked around him for a few moments, listened to the noise, saw the glitter of colour and personality. 'They seem to be having a good time.'

'Stoneleigh won't when he gets the bill.' Cranston's nostrils distended suddenly and he smiled grimly. 'The more so when he learns it's all for nothing.'

'How do you mean?'

Cranston looked at Eric Ward again, weighing him up and, eventually, discarding him as a country innocent. He shook his head. 'The Honourable Antony Stoneleigh isn't unknown to us. He's beaten a path to our doors at the bank; this isn't the first scheme he's come up with. This time ... well, I advised Sir John we ought to have a look at it. But ...'

'He's been to you before?'

Cranston sipped disdainfully at his orange juice. 'That young man is a man in a hurry to get somewhere. A youngest son, I believe, with a burning desire to make a name — and money — for himself. A man of vision, and ideas. The trouble is, the visions are largely chimerical and the ideas impractical. In a good company, as a pusher, he might make a career for himself; as a salesman he might excel — once he learns to read people a bit more sensibly. But none of that suits the Honourable Antony's ego. He wants to be the big man. The trouble is, he isn't big enough. Certainly not to con Sir John.'

Eric Ward hesitated. 'Stoneleigh was hoping to get financial support from the bank.'

Cranston shook his head. 'Unlikely. I've had a look at it. I don't say the idea isn't sound, but the capital investment programme would have to be huge, so the only way it would be viable, this Seaham thing, would be by way of Government support — and *that's* out as far as Whitehall is concerned — or through a much less ambitious attempt. In other words, if Stoneleigh wants out of the mess he's burying himself into, he needs to sell sixty per cent of the deal to one of the big consortia. And even then he'd have to kiss goodbye to a large part of his investment.'

'Would he be able to interest one of the big firms?'

'I think so. My guess, for what it's worth—' and the way Cranston said it made it clear he thought his guess extremely valuable — 'my guess is that he's already negotiating. I've heard a whisper in the City. But to come through with that one he'll have to keep his coat tails clean, and show that his present financial base is strong. I'm not so sure it is, after a look at his books.' Cranston grunted. He made a vague gesture with his glass. 'But look at all this. When will these young hopefuls come to realize that sprats of this kind are irrelevant if you want to catch the big mackerel? They just don't work. The bait has got to be a real one — a commitment to a project, backed by sound forward planning, financial infrastructure, and the ability to convince on the expert side.'

'I've heard Stoneleigh. He can be convincing.'

Pityingly, Cranston said, 'Only to the green and folly-ridden, the incautious and the gullible. And, maybe, the lunatic gambling fringe. Sir John counts himself among none of those groups. No; Stoneleigh will have to work harder than this to get the City to back him — and throwing a party is no way out of the mire.'

'You say he really lacks a sound financial base?'

'A base with depth. Something solid. He's picked up small investors, but they won't carry him through to a completion of the Seaham project as he envisages it. No, he needs a base. What he ought to do, in my view, is marry money. Best way out of *his* problem.'

Eric Ward glanced across the room to Antony Stoneleigh. He was talking to Anne Morcomb.

* * *

As the evening wore on some of the people at the party began to crumble under the effect of the heat, the noise and the alcohol. The company also took its toll. Eric kept himself in reasonable shape by taking a stroll outside on two further occasions, but the glimpses he obtained of Anne persuaded him that while she was enjoying herself, she also was not throwing herself into the thing as wildly as most of the others. Several young men, including Stoneleigh, paid her flattering attention for periods but she was managing to allow none to get attached to her, and on a couple of occasions he caught her glance: she appeared amused, but made no attempt to rejoin him as she moved among her acquaintances.

Colin Saxby did not wear well as the evening progressed, however. He was laying determined siege to the honey-haired lady, but there was an almost desperate air about his earnestness towards her and it had an impact upon his intake of alcohol.

He was drinking freely and it had made him noisier, slightly unsteady in his movements. Not that the woman with the honey-coloured hair appeared to notice, for if anything she was drinking faster and deeper than Colin Saxby was.

'He doesn't stand a chance,' Anne Morcomb said, suddenly appearing at Eric's elbow.

'He seems to be making an impact,' Eric disagreed.

'She's called Hilda. And she's already been smitten by someone else. You'll see.'

'Will I?'

'At close quarters. We'll be leaving soon.'

Eric Ward looked at her and raised his eyebrows. 'My place or yours?' he asked mockingly.

'Neither. But interesting.'

'And mysterious.'

She grinned and moved away to talk to a chinless representative of the Morpeth gentry. Eric looked around for the professional observer, Cranston, but he had already left the room. Eric would not be sorry to go himself.

Sir John Freshfield was holding court, but Antony Stoneleigh was taking up position at his elbow. He was accompanied by a girl who looked remarkably young — perhaps seventeen. As Eric watched, Stoneleigh managed to attract Freshfield's attention; there was a brief introduction and Freshfield engaged the young woman in a booming conversation and then Stoneleigh leaned forward and whispered something to the banker. Freshfield nodded, finished his drink and then backed out of the group, talking quickly, before he joined Stoneleigh and the two men walked away through a side door at the far end of the room. After a discreet interval, Eric noted, the young-looking girl also made her way out through the door.

The party was not thinning appreciatively and yet gaps seemed to have appeared. There was no sign of Joseph Francis now, nor some of the others of his group. Anne Morcomb was clearly discarding one of her admirers by quickly moving from one group to another, hovering on a fringe, avoiding conversational involvement and, moreover, taking a track that would inevitably bring her back to Eric Ward's side.

Five minutes later she was standing beside him. She looked up, grinning, and her eyes were bright, but it was not alcohol or excitement. Anticipation, maybe, but mixed with a tinge of nervousness. 'Right,' she said. 'Time to go.'

'Where?'

'I've got the directions.'

She led Eric towards the side door through which Stoneleigh and Sir John Freshfield had vanished.

It was only a short walk, Anne said, from the restaurant, so there was no need for the car. She was holding Eric's arm as they walked into the dark, cobbled side street, and her grip was tight. 'Where exactly are we going?' he asked.

She giggled. 'You'll see.'

'Anne—'

'Oh, all right. This is the reason why I asked you to accompany me. I wanted someone ... *reliable.*'

Somehow he gained little comfort from the word. 'That explains nothing.'

She laughed again, somewhat nervously. 'You clearly haven't heard of Sir John Freshfield's predilections.'

Eric thought suddenly of the young girl who had followed Stoneleigh and Freshfield out of the restaurant. 'Just exactly where *are* we going?' he demanded.

'Here.'

The door in the street was narrow and dark but the passageway behind the door was carpeted and the man who escorted them after Anne Morcomb mentioned Stoneleigh's name was well-dressed, if impassive. They climbed a flight of stairs and were led into what was clearly a private club of sorts, a large room scattered with perhaps twenty or thirty people. Colin Saxby was already there, with the honey-haired Hilda. So was Stoneleigh; so was Joseph Francis, a number of his cronies, and Sir John Freshfield, engaged in animated conversation with the young girl. They were all drinking, and the lights were low.

'Seems pretty tame,' Anne said disappointedly.

'Explain,' Eric insisted.

She pulled a face at him. 'Antony told me there'd be a special party laid on, apart from the other one. For Sir John. Asked me to come. I thought, not bloody likely, having heard what I've heard about him. But Antony said maybe I should bring someone reliable. So I did.'

'But why?'

'Because I wanted to *see,*' she said with a schoolgirl's excitement. 'Daddy kept a pretty tight rein, you know, up at Sedleigh Hall, and young men were vetted. I've never seen anything seedy, or ... well, *odd,* you know: they don't go in for orgies at the Young Conservatives, after all — at least, not sexy ones. So I thought—'

'You'd see how the other half behaves.' Eric Ward stared around him. During his time in the police force he had taken part in a few raids at clubs like this. There was nothing exceptionable about this club; others existed in the northern cities and elsewhere. You paid a great deal as one of the dirty coat brigade and got little enough for your money. Maybe Stoneleigh had laid on something special for Sir John, but it would still be the kind of thing that would probably lack both novelty and imagination.

'You really want to stay?' Eric asked. 'That's why I'm here,' she said. Resignedly, Eric settled down in an easy chair in the corner with Anne perched on the arm of the chair. Predictably the pattern established itself. More drinking, raucous voices, rumblings as stories were told, laughter breaking out in waves of sound. He watched while the splitting away began, couples retiring to the shaded corners of the large room, and then the red-waistcoated projectionist uncovering the machinery for the film. The lights flickered. down, the same old tawdry images flashed on the screen. It was just as Eric had known it would be: he glanced up to Anne from time to time, as she watched, but he could not see her face.

At the end of the film she turned to look at him. 'I don't think *that* was particularly funny.'

'It was supposed to be erotic,' he explained patiently. She grinned at him.

Between the film shows the relationships in the room developed. Sir John Freshfield had already disappeared: Eric knew there would be small, softly furnished rooms scattered through the building 'to accommodate those interested. Colin Saxby was clearly interested. He was making valiant efforts with Hilda, but the liquor she had imbibed was taking its toll and as Eric watched, Antony Stoneleigh came across and detached the girl from Colin Saxby's care. He spoke to her for a few minutes and she seemed to be hanging on every word; Eric suspected, nevertheless, she had not heard anything for she was very, very drunk. Colin Saxby glowered at them from the depths of an armchair, and began to rise when Stoneleigh started to lead Hilda across the room, gently, smiling. Then he sank back, and took a stiff shot of whisky. Stoneleigh and Hilda disappeared into the dim recesses of the room.

'I don't think he'll get much joy there,' Anne Morcomb whispered.

'I thought you were a young lady.'

'I am,' she said primly. 'That's why I brought you, as my protector.'

'Your protector thinks you ought to go home.'

She hesitated. 'In a little while. It's all pretty ... boring, really, isn't it? But something might happen.'

Eric Ward doubted it. He watched Colin Saxby. The man was drinking heavily. Eric wondered whether he had felt the pressure that Jack Saxby had clearly felt in court at Amos Saxby's theatrical announcement. It would be a reason for drinking the way he was — for there was something almost desperate about Colin Saxby's intake at the moment. Then, when Stoneleigh suddenly appeared again, alone, Eric guessed the truculence Saxby seemed to be developing would have a different origin — Hilda. For as Stoneleigh approached him Colin Saxby stood up, weaving slightly, and grabbed Stoneleigh by the arm. He began to speak, his mouth twisting angrily.

'Oh, oh,' Anne whispered. 'Looks like Antony's in trouble. But Hilda was always going to end up with him.'

Eric glanced at Anne curiously. Her tone was one of faint amusement. It seemed she cared little for what Antony Stoneleigh got up to; it was not the reaction Eric had expected.

Stoneleigh was now gripping Colin Saxby's wrist. He was talking, and fiercely; his words were enough to give Saxby pause. He was stepping back, Stoneleigh's contorted face thrusting into his, and then the argument was over as Antony Stoneleigh suddenly turned, stalked away back into the darkened areas of the room.

'Good luck, Hilda,' Anne Morcomb hummed under her breath. 'And bad luck, Saxby ... I think, Eric, I've had enough. If this is the nearest Newcastle can get to an orgy, no wonder Sir John Freshfield stays in London. Maybe I'll have to get a flat down there.'

'Young lady,' Eric admonished gravely, 'I'm astonished.' He rose, taking Anne's arm, just as Colin Saxby came lurching past.

'Ha! Ward, isn't it?' Saxby's bleary eyes wavered, trying to recognize Anne Morcomb. 'Fixed up, are you? Bloody poor party, 'sall I can say. And that bloody Stoneleigh ...' His features were contorted suddenly, and Eric realized that the loss of Hilda must have bitten deep into Colin Saxby's ego, for his eyes had become almost murderous. Then he swung his head, focusing on Eric Ward. 'You seen Jack? You advised him to lay-off yet?'

'I can't do that, Mr Saxby.'

'He ought to lay-off. The bastard. He ought to lay-off, nothing to be gained. Amos ... Amos'll skin him. *Amos* ought to lay-off, drop it all.' He peered vacantly at Anne Morcomb. 'Family business, you know; family affairs. Good that ... family affairs. Ha! Offer you a lift, my dear?'

'No, thank you,' Anne said soberly. 'I already have a lift. Mr Ward—'

'Ward. Yes. You told my brother he ... he could go ahead, didn't you? Bad advice, bad. Very dangerous. Can't win, you know, can't win not with old Amos ...' He shook his head, muttering, then looked at Anne again. 'Don't want a lift? Got Sam's car, you know. Take you wherever. .. No? Well, then ...' He shook his head and began to walk away towards the door.

'Do you think he'll make it?'

'I don't intend trying to stop him,' Eric said. 'In his mood, he's not far from the edge of violence. And if he's parked near Grey's, he's likely to get stopped anyway. This time in the morning there'll be a doorman keeping his eyes open. Reputation of the club, you know.'

They walked out into the cobbled street, Colin Saxby somewhere ahead of them in the darkness. It was a soft night, the sky a deep blue-black colour, with hints of a still distant dawn fading the distant horizon. They walked past the restaurant and returned to Eric's car; silently he drove Anne back to Montague Court.

As he drove his thoughts returned to Colin Saxby: the man had clearly been drunk, and bothered about his loss of the honey-blonde to Antony Stoneleigh, but his conversation had surprisingly turned to the Holton Hill Farm affair. It was clear that the wounds caused by that business were deep-scored among the Saxby family; strictly speaking, it had nothing to do with Colin Saxby in that it was a quarrel between the old man and his youngest son, Jack, but the other two sons had been drawn deeply into it and stances were being taken.

And in Colin Saxby's view, Jack stood no chance against Amos Saxby — even though Colin himself had clearly won, on two separate occasions — first in his refusal to accept a mere tenancy of Brookfield Farm when he was still in the Army, and later, when he had sold the farm and used the money to invest elsewhere.

They reached Montague Court; Eric got out and walked with Anne to the lift. She was quiet; he wondered briefly whether she was thinking of Antony Stoneleigh with the blonde Hilda. They entered the lift and it rushed them to the top floor. Anne unlocked her door and walked in, leaving the door open, and obviously expecting him to enter. Eric hesitated, glanced at his watch. It was almost two in the morning. 'Close the door behind you,' Anne called mockingly, and feeling foolish, he entered. She had already taken off her coat, and was headed for the kitchen.

He stood by the window, looking out over the city again as she busied herself making some coffee. He heard her come in, set the cups down, but he did not turn. After a moment she stood beside him. 'Thanks for taking me . .. and suffering me.'

'It wasn't much of a show, was it?' he said.

'Maybe it was a piece of foolishness I needed to get out of my system. There's a little voyeurism in us all, and I was

... curious. I'm not curious any more. At least, not about the goings-on of the likes of Sir John Freshfield.'

'And what about Antony Stoneleigh?'

'I never was interested in his predilections.'

Something that Eric Ward refused to recognize as relief moved him. Gruffly he said, 'Did you put any money into that Seaham project of his?'

'No. I wasn't persuaded. Not that I don't think it would be a good thing, but after I'd spoken to my accountant I had some doubts.'

'I think he advised you well.'

'What do you mean?'

'I gather that Freshfield won't be supporting the project — and that means Stoneleigh might be in some trouble. He could stand to lose his stake.'

She moved restlessly and he caught a hint of her perfume. 'I don't think he himself has too much money tied up in it ... at least, that's what my accountant says. But others ... there are other investors who've put a lot in. He's likely to be a bit unpopular if the project fails.'

'Then he's going to be unpopular.'

She was silent for a while. At last she said, 'He never roused my curiosity the way you did.'

'Curiosity?'

'I know what makes Antony tick. I know his sales talk, his badinage, I can recognize his flirting for what it is — which is more than *you* can, I suspect. In fact, you have a somewhat direct and simple view of people, don't you?'

'I wasn't aware of it.'

'Well, you have. And something else. A kind of self-centred control: you look at other people, look at yourself, undertake some kind of reasoned computation, and reach a decision. It's all a bit cold, really.'

'But, possibly, necessary.'

'Why?'

'It avoids complications.'

'Of a personal kind?'

'Yes,' Eric said.

'Is that why I haven't seen you for two years?'

There was something leaden in his chest. He could not look at her. There were dangers in the air, in the atmosphere, and they were closing in on him in a manner he felt irresistible. 'Two years ... there was no reason for you to consult the firm.'

'You know damned well that wasn't what I meant.' There was no fire, no rancour in her tone; it even held a hint of amusement.

He hesitated. 'I think it's time I went.'

'Running again?'

'Again?' he countered.

'The way you did two years ago.'

He looked at her then, stared into her eyes and felt his resolve crumbling. He shook his head. 'I'm twenty years older than you, Anne.'

'I'm alone in the flat.'

'I'm a crusty old bachelor, only half fit, committed to building a new career for myself—'

'You could stay the night, avoid the journey home.'

'I'd better go. It's stupid to think—'

'Then don't think,' she said and she reached for him and his confusion was total, his resolve non-existent, and she felt as he had always known she would feel, warm, soft, and the taste of her was a compound of excitement and relief that he knew he would never forget.

The coffee remained untasted in the cups.

* * *

Dawn lit the sky with a spreading gold stain as he walked along the Quayside, reluctant yet to return to Wylam. There was much to think about, so much to explain, but his thoughts were confused and he could not find the words to tell her. Everything had changed and yet nothing had changed: the gulf still remained between them, made up of her youth and

90

his middle age. But over and above that there was his lack of future. He had known for some time the truth with regard to his feelings for her — he was in love with her, however much he might fight against it, deride it for its impracticality, sneer at it for its hopelessness. And she loved him — he knew that now, after tonight. But what could he offer her beyond the one certainty, of blindness? Nothing. A man with crippled eyes, with a career that had hardly even got started. It was no way to begin a marriage.

Her solution would be a simple one: she had money enough for both of them, there were the Morcomb estates; he need not worry about his illness or his future — the best doctors, a life of relaxed lack of need. But it was a solution he could not bring himself to accept. He was his own man and he needed to carve out his *own* solutions to his problems. He could not burden her with them and retain his self-respect; and there was the possibility that in time they would weigh her down, destroy what he now accepted lay between them.

He knew it was still the right thing to do, in spite of tonight; it was still right to walk away, if he now could.

He was aware of activity near Pudding Chare as he walked — cars, blue lights flashing, a street accident, ambulances. He turned, walked away, back to his car, to nurse his anxieties and his longings and consider for the hundredth time how different it all could have been but for the pain gnawing at the nerve ends behind his eyes.

He thought no more of the accident near the Quayside. Not until late the next afternoon, when the news filtered through to the office. A man had been killed in a hit-and-run accident near Pudding Chare.

The man's name was Jack Saxby.

CHAPTER 4

Freddie Jenkins was a big man, square-set in his body, muscles turning to fat, sandy hair now thinning badly at his temples but his eyes still lively and twinkling, and his wide mouth as ready to smile as ever. Eric Ward had known him for twenty years, ever since he had joined the Northumbria Force, and he rated Freddie more highly than some of the hierarchy. Freddie Jenkins was now a Superintendent in the Criminal Investigation Department, but he had had the ability to go higher. Somehow, chances had seemed to pass him by and lesser men had been promoted. It might have been due to a certain lack of respect for authority he occasionally displayed; it might have been the result of some of the methods he employed from time to time — a thick ear instead of a charge sheet, a physical warning instead of a prosecution. He had been a tearaway as a young man; he had mellowed now, and had developed a comfortable paunch.

Eric said so.

Freddie Jenkins patted it complacently. 'It's the sedentary life,' he explained, beaming. 'I tell you, Eric, they got some real whizz-kids in CID now, and the old hands like me, well, we can just sit back most of the time, like. Except every now and then.'

'You were always too damned nosy to take a back seat,' Eric chided him.

'Aye, well, maybe you're right.' Superintendent Jenkins grinned. 'That's why I'm here, I suppose.'

'I thought it was unlikely to be a friendly call.'

'Oh, that as well. Always nice to see old friends who've fallen into the easy life. Nice office, pretty secretary, good salary.'

'And a healthy curiosity,' Eric said, 'as to why a busy super should take the trouble to call in.'

Freddie Jenkins scratched his bulbous nose. 'You said I was always a bit ... inquisitive. You'll remember I was also a bit, shall we say, intuitive?'

'A Welsh trait, you used to say. Hunches. So what have you come to see me about?'

Jenkins smiled. 'Don't you offer any kind of hospitality around here?'

'I can arrange coffee.'

'If you've nothing better ...' After Eric had asked Philippa to bring in some coffee he went on, 'The hunch is that a certain hit-and-run the other evening isn't quite ... right. The boys are inclined to write it off as just that — a drunk, late at night, hitting a pedestrian. But me, I'm not so sure.'

'You're talking about Jack Saxby?'

'I am.'

'Why the hunch?'

Freddie Jenkins considered for a moment. 'Time of night. About two-thirty in the morning. What was he doing near Pudding Chare? And he was hit fair and square, you know — no glancing blow. Crushed skull, pelvic damage, the lot. Never stood a chance. And no sign of the car.'

'That's to be expected,' Eric said, 'though you'll have checked the garages.'

'Throughout the region. But I got a *feelin'* about this one, and it leaves me uneasy.'

'And you think I can help in some way.'

Freddie Jenkins stared directly at Eric. 'He was a client of yours.'

Philippa bustled in with some coffee, remarking brightly that she had already been making it when she saw Mr Jenkins arrive. A conspiratorial wink at the superintendent, and she was gone.

'Always could charm them,' Eric remarked. 'But ... the fact that Saxby was my client is neither here nor there. Any connection—'

'Ah, well, we don't know about that yet do we, until we talk about it, like?'

'I can assure you—'

'You can't.' Jenkins grinned. 'Not when I hear you were in his brother's company shortly before Jack Saxby was killed.'

Eric was silent. He watched as the big Welshman reached for the sugar bowl and ladled heaped teaspoonfuls into his coffee. He shook his head. 'You think Jack Saxby was murdered.'

'My colleagues don't.'

'But you ... have a hunch.'

Jenkins stirred his coffee. 'That's right. And let's start with a bit of corroboration. You were with Colin Saxby that night?'

'Not exactly *with* him. In the same ... party.'

Freddie Jenkins's grin became expansive and he twinkled his eyes at Eric. 'Didn't know you went in for that kind of thing. Legal life must have changed you. Cheap thrills and blue film shows ... oh yes, we know about that club, as you'll have guessed. But no chance of a raid that night, of course, with the bigwigs there. But *you*, Eric ...'

'I was ... accompanying someone,' Eric said stiffly.

'I bet. Anyway, never mind. You confirm Colin Saxby's presence. Like to tell me how the evening went? In relation to him, I mean.'

'Colin Saxby?' Eric raised his eyebrows and shrugged. 'He got pretty smashed, I can tell you that.'

'Gimme an outline.'

'Well, he'd had a fair amount to drink at Grey's — there was a party there for Sir John Freshfield.'

'So I gather. Thrown by this Stoneleigh character.'

'That's right. Then, when we were at the private club, Saxby was still drinking pretty heavily. He had got involved with a woman called Hilda, but had his nose put out of joint by Stoneleigh, who whisked her off—'

'I get the picture. Leaving Saxby to cry in his beer.'

'Champagne.'

'Still ends in a hangover. So what happened then?'

Eric Ward sipped his coffee. 'Nothing, really. As you might imagine, Saxby had a few words with Antony Stoneleigh over the girl, but Stoneleigh and the girl then disappeared and shortly after that we decided to go. Saxby left just ahead of us.'

'What time would that be?'

'Just before two.'

'And Saxby ... he looked pretty far gone?'

'I'd have said so. I wasn't sure whether he should have been allowed to drive.'

Freddie Jenkins's head came up. He stared at Eric unwinkingly for several seconds. Then, casually, he asked, 'Did you see him to his car?'

'No. He walked ahead of us; I didn't see him.'

'You didn't see him drive away?' Eric shook his head.

Freddie Jenkins sighed. 'Ah, well. According to Colin Saxby, it would have been an impossibility anyway.'

'How do you mean?'

'He claims someone stole his car from outside Grey's that night.'

It was Eric's turn to stare. 'I hadn't heard that.'

'No, well ... The fact is, the duty sergeant got a report in the early hours not from Colin Saxby, but from his brother Sam. It would seem Sam Saxby's car had been stolen, when it was in the custody or care of Colin. When I heard about it I thought I'd better get the whole story.'

'And?' Eric prompted.

'It would seem that it was quite a social night for the Saxbys. Colin was due at Grey's — Sam and Jack Saxby were attending a monthly farmers' orgy — yes, believe it! It seems they have some kind of club going; this time the excuse for the meeting was a discussion on farm subsidies, but it's strictly stag and there's time for some gungho drinking afterwards, apparently. So, there's all three of them fixed up for a night out — and so is the old man.'

'Amos Saxby?'

'He's at a meeting of some kind or other in Sunderland, don't you know, and not certain what time he'll be getting back to Morpeth. The gay widower, looks like.'

'So what about this car thing?'

Freddie Jenkins finished his coffee with gusto. 'Colin Saxby had his own transport but the distributor packed up on him. I've checked that, incidentally, and the car is in a garage at the moment. So he has a word with brother Sam, who agrees to go to Newcastle with Colin. Sam gets dropped at the farmer's do, bottom of Grainger Street, and Colin gets use of the car to drive the short distance up to Grey's. The idea was that Colin would pick up Sam later, bring him home. He was also supposed to stay sober, to do the chauffeuring.'

'He hardly did that,' Eric commented.

'So it seems. Anyway, Sam Saxby reports his car stolen, we get the story but it's a bit garbled.'

'In what way?'

Freddie Jenkins shook his head. 'Colin Saxby claims he came out about two and there's no car waiting for him. Now in those circumstances I'd have phoned the police straight away — or at least made enquiries at Grey's. Colin Saxby did neither — he merely walked down to Grainer Street. He says he was a bit fuddled with drink; couldn't think straight; concluded Sam had collected the car and was waiting for him; couldn't even be sure what the arrangements were any more. So he walks down, and there's no sign of Sam Saxby. He'd left the farmer's shindig.'

Eric looked at the superintendent thoughtfully. 'To look for Colin?'

'That's *Sam's* story. Because his brother was late with the car.'

'They finally met?'

'They did. Top of Grey Street. About three in the morning. Amazing, isn't it?' The sarcasm was not lost on Eric. 'Possible,' he said.

'Yeah, but *imagine* the scene,' Jenkins said. 'There are the three brothers wandering around Newcastle, separately, in the early hours of the morning, all carrying a load of booze, not seeing each other — and one of them gets killed, just like that!'

'You didn't explain about Jack Saxby,' Eric said.

'Oh, didn't I tell you?' Jenkins asked sarcastically. 'Nobody seems quite sure, but someone *thinks* there was a phone-call for Jack Saxby. It was made about two in the morning; there or thereabouts. It's enough to send him out on the streets, and wandering down towards the Quayside, and Pudding Chare. Where, fancy it, he gets crushed by a car; hit-and-run. Doesn't it smell to you, Eric?'

'I see what you mean.' Eric was silent for a little while.

Freddie Jenkins watched him, and then said, 'And then there's the matter of the car keys.'

'To Sam Saxby's car?'

'No less. Someone had pinched the car, *Colin* says. But when he met Sam at three, as far as he can remember he gave the car keys to Sam. *Colin* says. But that ain't how *Sam* recalls it. Albeit imperfectly. His story is he doesn't recall Colin giving them to him. Rather, they just argued about the loss of the car and then reported it. He's got a spare set of keys — but no originals. And a fuzzy evening was had by all, don't you agree?'

Eric nodded. 'Even so, I'm not very clear why you're telling me all this.'

'Oh, I know lawyers. Feel they got to protect their clients' interests and all that. So I thought I'd fill you in on all the background. Jack Saxby — dead from hit-and-run. I got that. Brothers Sam and Colin drunk as noodles, they say, in the same town, but no keys to the car, they say, and car gone missing. Amos, their old man, wandering somewhere between Sunderland and Newcastle in his own car around about that time. So, I ask myself, were they a happy family?' His eyes fixed on Eric and he smiled thinly. 'And a little bird tells me no. Same little bird says, go see Eric Ward. Always was a helpful character, Eric Ward. So I'm here. So be helpful.'

'I don't know how I can.'

'You know all right, but you want time to think. So—' Jenkins waved a generous hand '—'take some time.'

Eric Ward shook his head doubtfully. 'I'm not sure what there is to tell ... what information I can give you.' He rose uneasily from behind his desk and walked across to the window, looked out across the city. 'You'll have to be more specific.'

'So I'll be more specific. There's bad blood in the family.'

Eric turned and stared at the detective-superintendent. 'Are you suggesting that one of the Saxby family was implicated in Jack Saxby's death?'

'Hey, come on, Eric.' Freddie Jenkins spread his hands wide in innocence. 'Have I said anything? I just gave you some facts ... and now I'm asking you to give me some, in return. But did I *say* anything?' Eric Ward hesitated, then returned to his desk thoughtfully. 'All right, there's bad blood.'

'What's it about?'

'The fact that the old man — Amos looked after two of the sons but not the third. The signs are he set out deliberately, with his wife, to undo something that had been arranged earlier ... the sale of a farm to Jack Saxby. That's about it.'

'And Jack Saxby was taking the old man to law?'

'Correct.'

'So where do the brothers fit in?'

'They don't.' As he saw a spasm of frustration cross the superintendent's features, Eric added, 'It was your supposition, not mine. You asked for facts. I gave them.'

'They're not involved?'

'Well ...' Eric conceded, 'maybe Sam Saxby is. He witnessed a conveyance of the farm from Ellen Saxby to Amos; there's a suspicion he might have colluded ... might have worked with his parents to do Jack Saxby down.'

'Conspiracy?'

'That's the word.'

'I'm more interested in Colin Saxby.'

'As far as I can make out ...' Eric began, and then hesitated, uncertain whether he should proceed.

'Go on.' Jenkins urged.

'There might be nothing to it,' Eric said slowly. 'And in a sense, it's only hearsay. And from Sam Saxby, at that.'

'You're keeping me in suspense.'

'Colin Saxby ... before he went to the Army he was courting the woman who became Jack Saxby's wife.'

Superintendent Jenkins stared at Eric Ward, his mouth opening in mock surprise. 'Well, well ... tell me more.'

Eric shrugged. 'I'm not certain there's much more to tell. Amos Saxby didn't care for the courtship with Sandra and had a shouting match with Colin. He imposed his personality upon his son and Colin then shoved off to get out of his way, joined the Army. While he was away it seems Jack Saxby might have stepped into his shoes—'

'*Might* have?'

'Slip of the tongue. I meant did.'

Superintendent Jenkins shook his head. 'No. Lawyers are careful with words. You especially. Let's have it out, Eric.'

Eric Ward shook his head irritably. 'It's only a feeling. I've only met the woman once, with her husband. It's merely that I got the impression ... she had such a dissatisfied air, and seemed to treat Jack Saxby with a degree of contempt—'

'In front of you?'

'That's right.'

'So when you heard,' Jenkins surmised wonderingly, 'that Jack Saxby wasn't Sandra's *first* choice, and tied it in with her dissatisfied air, you wondered ...'

'Nothing specific,' Eric insisted.

'But you still wondered whether she was still hankering after the one that got away. He — Colin Saxby — he's not married?'

'No. Still feels himself a bit of an adventurer. Life in the Army unsettled him for farming, so though Amos made over Brookfield to him, he sold it later and now plays the markets, I understand.'

'With Sandra still sighing in the wings, and brother Jack locked in litigation with Amos, the old lady dying ... it all makes for quite a thick soup, doesn't it?'

'I think we're exaggerating the importance of some of this.'

'But the old man was a bit outspoken in court, I understand,' Jenkins said. 'Said he'd see Jack in hell, or words to that effect.'

Eric Ward leaned back in his chair and folded his arms. 'Don't read too much into that, either,' he said. 'Amos Saxby has a talent for the theatrical. He *projects* a bit. It was done quite deliberately to hurt Jack.'

'Even though the method of his announcement would also strike at his other two sons,' Jenkins mused. 'Well, you say theatrical, I say there's a streak of vicious carelessness there too. Hmmm. Very interesting. All right, Eric, thanks, it all helps build up a picture — even if the edges remain hazy. But still one puzzle. *Why?*'

'Why did Amos Saxby have it in for Jack?' Eric shook his head. 'I don't know. I have a suspicion that Colin and Sam Saxby know the reason, but it's family business, and they're holding those cards to their chests. But of one thing I'm pretty sure. It concerns something that must have happened fairly recently.'

'How do you know?'

'Ellen Saxby created the option to purchase in 1974. She'd held the farm since 1969. So, she and Amos were still well disposed towards Jack a few years ago. He did something then, fairly recently, to upset them. He — or maybe Sandra

— caused a rift in the family and Amos and Ellen worked out this ploy to pull the farm back from him.'

'Maybe they needed the money sunk in the farm?'

'No. They were well enough off. Amos has money, it seems, enough to keep him in comfort at the Old Vicarage in Morpeth.'

'So something happened ...' Freddie Jenkins mused for a little while, then suddenly slapped his large hands on his knees and rose to his feet. 'All very interesting. And maybe important ... but still indecisive. So, keep in touch, hey? Anything you come across you think might be of assistance, you let me know.' He paused at the door, looked back at Eric. 'Two brothers, wandering around the city late at night. Would have been better for Colin Saxby if he'd managed to get his hands on the girl at the party, wouldn't it? Kept him busy at the important time, when Jack was killed.'

Eric shrugged. 'I don't think she'd have kept anyone busy for long — she was too damned drunk.'

Jenkins grinned. 'Never objected to that too much myself. What's a snore or two among close friends? Thanks again, lad; keep in touch.'

After the door had banged behind him Eric sat quietly in his chair for several minutes as the half-formed questions moved around in his head, a kaleidoscope of facts and theories, shifting patterns of light and shade, motives and reasons, knowledge and misunderstandings. In one sense it was all none of his business; he had certain links with the family, but the legal base was limited and clearly had nothing to do with murder. On the other hand, Sandra Saxby had already rung to make an appointment with him, and he had little doubt what it would mean. If Amos Saxby were to be brought to heel over the matter of Holton Hill Farm, it was still necessary that Eric should discover more of the background, to discover what had finally caused the rift between parents and son. For if the battle were to be recommenced against the executors to Jack Saxby's estate, it would not be easy to make the charge of conspiracy stick

... unless a motive could be shown, a reason strong enough to demonstrate why Amos, Ellen and, possibly, Sam Saxby should have banded together in an unfair manner to deprive Jack Saxby of his legal rights.

Eric Ward reached for the telephone and buzzed for Philippa.

'Get me Jackie Parton,' he said.

* * *

A desultory attempt had been made to clean up part of the river area west of Newcastle. A team of youngsters had descended under a Work Experience project to get rid of the rusting hulks, the industrial debris, the broken-slatted fencing, and change the general air of depressed inactivity that the open ground possessed. But the mudflats were still there, and the beached boats seemed lost as they lay on their sides, gunwales stained with mud, and there were already graffiti and other signs of vandalism appearing on the three huts erected as boathouses by the river.

A mist girdled the river, low-lying, cloaking the far banks, but the line of the Durham hills was clear enough. The Hydraulic Engine pub standing above the mudflats, gave a good view across to the hills and in the old days the red stain of the Consett iron works had marked the sky. Now, as Eric stood in the window, looking out across the river, the sky was grey and still above the rattling stream of traffic that ground along the road west, along the river bank, diverted by road works, bringing back a spurious sense of life and activity to an area that had long since been denuded of people and work.

But the Hydraulic Engine itself still had its devoted clientele: the old men who had lived in Scotswood as children and seen it destroyed; the Irish immigrants who came to work and stayed to drink; the people who came for a touch of atmosphere in a pub that refused to change its face or ways; and the fringe people, the well-dressed, well-heeled individuals who never seemed to have a regular job but had contacts, and information, and capers that kept them in beer and cigarettes, champagne and brandy. It was also Jackie Parton's favourite pub.

Eric Ward never felt entirely at ease in the Hydraulic Engine, for he was known as an ex-policeman, and the opprobrium which that attracted still remained with him. Jackie Parton was in a quite different situation: there were few pubs throughout Tyneside where he was not recognized and welcomed, for in his years as a jockey on the northern tracks he had attracted an immense local following, not only among the punting fraternity but also in local pride and legend. A Scotswood lad who had fought his way out of the back-to-back houses down by the river, he had become the King of Tyneside with his flamboyant, successful riding and his reckless spending. Even his fall, when he was but thirty, still provoked violent arguments: a stewards' enquiry had announced he was involved in illegal betting syndicates but a strong body of opinion declared the matter had been rigged against him. It was a view even more hotly contested when his racing days ended with his being found, badly beaten, down by the Quayside. He never spoke about it, but rumour had it that his problems had really begun when he had refused the local gangs the chance of a killing at Wetherby. He was made an example of, to bring lesser riders into line. It ended his career, but not his popularity.

Now, he did occasional work for Eric Ward and others. Investigative agents were often retired policemen like Eric himself, who knew the law, procedures, and had a local understanding. Jackie Parton had more to offer — an unrivalled acquaintance with the underworld, the sporting world, and the wealthy on Tyneside, for he had spent freely, lived well in his day, and the upper crust of the racing fraternity still knew and accepted him. Even so, he still liked his pint, and preferred to take it in the Hydraulic Engine.

He had listened in silence while Eric Ward had sketched out for him the background to the Saxby affair. He had heard of the death of Jack Saxby, knew of the whisper that it could have been a deliberate hit-and-run, but there had been no information in Scotswood or Byker or anywhere else on the fringes that touched upon the death of Amos Saxby's youngest son.

'Do you think you can do your own check of the garages?' Eric had asked the little man.

'Could do ... the doubtful ones, you mean.' Jackie Parton had fingered his scarred lip thoughtfully. 'The police will tie up the legit ones.'

'Give it a try.'

'And what else?'

Eric had tried to explain, but knew that he was leaving the ex-jockey an extremely difficult task, for there was little or nothing to go on. In essence, he had to ask him to find out *anything* of interest concerning the Saxbys, but that could amount to very little, for it was almost certain there would be little to discover, publicly, of a family squabble.

'But there might be something,' Eric suggested.

The little man's grey eyes were doubtful. 'Don't know too many among the farming community. The clubs, now, that's different. But whispers from *farmers* ... it just don't happen, Eric.'

'Something might turn up. In essence, I want to find out just why Amos and Ellen Saxby turned so positively against their youngest son.'

Jackie Parton had promised to do what he could.

Now, after the little man had gone and the darkness reached out to shroud the Durham hills above the faintly gleaming river, Eric waited a little while longer to do his own bit of questioning. For there was one person who had remained evasive, and it was time he was brought to book.

Joseph had not been happy about further questions, when Eric had been to see him, and had almost insisted that Eric should not further involve Paul Francis in the matter. But there were questions to be asked, and it was Eric who was handling the Saxby affair. So, in his view, the decision was his.

At seven that evening he drove across to Gosforth to call on Paul Francis, at his flat.

* * *

The barrister was not exactly pleased to see him: that was obvious; Eric suspected, also, that Joseph had warned his son that he might be getting a call. Clearly, Paul Francis had decided to take the bull by the horns. At the entrance to his flat he smiled a welcome, invited Eric in, offered him a drink, and when Eric accepted a soft drink, settled back into an expensive, deep armchair and enquired after his health.

'How are you, Eric?'

'Well enough.'

'That's not what Joseph tells me. Talk of an operation, isn't there?'

'I haven't decided yet.'

There was a glitter in Paul Francis's eyes as he watched Eric over the rim of his whisky glass. 'If it comes to an operation, that'll cause problems for you, won't it? With the firm, I mean.'

Eric had no doubt what he meant: who would want to employ a blind solicitor? 'We'll see about that once I've had the operation ... if I have it.'

'Yes, it must be a fearful decision to take. So much pressure for you ... Did you enjoy the party the other night? You were with the Morcomb girl later, weren't you?'

'I escorted her.'

The eyes glittered again, mockingly: it was a track Eric, with his own feelings and emotions so confused, was not desirous of walking down. 'I came along to see you about the Saxby business,' he said shortly.

Paul Francis raised an elegant eyebrow and smoothed his thin cheeks. 'Saxby? I thought you'd briefed Charlie Dawson. Something gone wrong?'

Eric's mouth tightened. Paul was being deliberately evasive: he knew perfectly well there was no question of a brief in the matter . 'You'll have heard Jack Saxby was killed in a hit-and-run accident.'

'Yes, I had,' Paul Francis said carelessly. 'But that shouldn't change issues. There's his executors to sue, I suppose.'

Joseph Francis *had* been talking to him. Grimly Eric went on, 'It does make things that little bit more difficult, as you'll appreciate. Jack Saxby was obviously central to the case, and now he isn't around to instruct me. His widow will be calling to see me tomorrow, but I don't know how far she can help. I have a feeling *you* can help.'

'Me, dear boy?' Paul Francis smiled thinly.

'More than you have.'

'Can't see how.'

'Start by being a bit more honest about the Saxby files and the option to purchase.'

The smile vanished. Paul Francis suddenly looked petulant and he drank his whisky quickly, then glared at Eric. 'You're suggesting I've been less than honest—'

'*I know* you have,' Eric said wearily. 'Let's cut out the fencing. You never liked it at Francis, Shaw and Elder. You didn't like my arrival; you didn't like working for your father; and it all spilled over into your work. You weren't *interested,* and that lack of interest showed in the level of competence you displayed.'

'I don't need to take that sort of comment!'

The anger was forced, and lacked solid foundation. Eric looked into Paul Francis's eyes and saw the doubt and uncertainty there. 'You'll take it, Paul, because you know I'm telling the truth. And you're out of it now; making a good fist of it in chambers. You've found your niche and things are working out for you. But I've still got a job to do — albeit a less glamorous one than yours, and subject to more drudgery.'

Somewhat mollified, but still sullen, Paul Francis said, 'I still don't see how I can help you.'

Eric Ward reached in his pocket. He had noted down the last transactions on the Saxby index of files. He read them out aloud. Paul Francis rose and poured himself another drink.

'Now then,' Eric asked, 'the first file is on the 1969 Holton Hill Farm conveyance to Ellen Saxby. You won't have dealt with that—'

'Certainly not.'

'Nor the second one that year: the conveyance of Eastgate Farm to Samuel Saxby.'

'No.'

Eric paused, eyeing Paul Francis challengingly. 'But you *did* draw up the option to purchase, in Jack Saxby's favour, didn't you?'

There was a short silence. Paul Francis inspected his drink but his eyes were not still, flickering, disturbed; he grimaced, baring his teeth, nibbled at his lip. 'I ... I might have.'

'You'd remember if you did.'

'I'm not sure.'

'You're *sure.*' Eric insisted softly and the pale eyes flickered at him, angry, but nervous too and then Paul Francis nodded. 'All right, dammit, I drew up the option — Ellen Saxby instructed me herself. She rang me, asked me to go out to the Old Vicarage, and we dealt with the matter there.'

'So why the hell didn't you register the option thereafter?' Eric demanded.

'One of the legal executives—'

'Oh, come off it, Paul!' Eric said angrily. 'You had the file; it would have taken a phone call, then a letter of registration—'

'All right, dammit, all right! Have it your own way. I just *forgot* to register the bloody thing, that's all, I just forgot. Hell's flames, we all make mistakes from time to time, don't we?'

'Some more critical than others,' Eric said hotly. 'All right, never mind.' He paused, thinking. 'Now the next access to the Saxby files occurred when Samuel Saxby wanted to resolve a wayleave problem over Eastgate Farm. You handled that.'

'Yes.'

Paul Francis was uneasy again. Eric waited, letting the tension mount between them. 'All right,' he said, 'what files — actual files — would you have taken up on that issue? When you prepared the brief to counsel you would, presumably, have needed the 1969 conveyance of Eastgate Farm itself.'

'Of course.'

'And the Holton Hill Farm conveyance?'

'No.'

'But they could have been in the same bundle.'

Paul Francis hesitated. 'They ... they could have been.'

'You mean they were.'

Temper flashed into Paul Francis's tone. 'All right, they were! I don't see—'

'All four files are missing from the office, Paul. I want to know why. I can accept it was an oversight on your part that might have occasioned it, but for God's sake tell me straight about it, and stop prevaricating. What the hell happened to those files?'

'I don't damned well know.' Paul Francis bit his lip nervously. 'I think ...'

'Go on.'

'The last occasion ... I'd gone out to Eastgate Farm. I discussed with Sam Saxby the proposed action — though it never came off in fact, even though we briefed counsel, because there was a settlement out of court. We ... we had a drink to celebrate, and Sam Saxby was most ... affable. He seemed very grateful that the whole thing had been dealt with so satisfactorily. It was a pleasant evening, and we cracked a bottle of wine ...

'And?'

Paul Francis's face twisted uncertainly. 'I can't be sure. It was a long time ago, and I can't really remember, but like I told Joseph, I think there's the possibility that I left the files at Eastgate Farm.'

Eric Ward stared at the barrister. 'You *think* you left them there? Didn't you check, afterwards?'

Francis shook his head in irritation. 'Check what? It was one of a number of issues I was dealing with at the time. And the matter was finished. Moreover, it wasn't long after that I left the firm, and I had a hell of a lot on my mind.' He looked up defiantly, his eyes suddenly challenging Eric. 'Besides, what difference does it make? We've no God-given or legal right to those papers. They belong in fact to the clients, and if they've ended up with the family, who haven't seen fit to return them, we can't *demand* their return. They are only working papers, in our safe keeping. So what the hell!'

It wasn't the point, but there was nothing to be gained by arguing with Paul Francis. Wearily, Eric Ward shook his head. 'All right, Paul, let's leave it at that. I don't think Sam Saxby should be holding on to papers rightly belonging to another member of the family, but let's overlook that for now. It might yet be of some help to me if you can tell me what was in the files.'

'After three years? Aw, come *on!*'

Perhaps it was unreasonable, but there was still the question regarding Amos Saxby's motivations to be dealt with, and the reason why Ellen Saxby had turned against her youngest son. 'The 1969 papers,' Eric asked, 'the ones relating to the conveyance of Holton Hill Farm — what did they contain?'

Paul Francis shrugged coldly. 'What does any conveyancing file contain? Details of searches, contract of sale—'

'Root of title?'

'That's right. All the usual stuff.'

'Did you do the root of title yourself?' Eric asked.

'Yes. It was pretty straightforward. It had been left to Mrs Saxby by a cousin. Can't remember his name ...'

'Jennings,' Eric supplied. 'Frank Jennings.'

'Well, you always had a better memory than me,' Paul Francis conceded. 'So there was the usual material there; notification of death, probate of the will, payment of legacies, supporting affidavits and other correspondence from the Jennings solicitors—'

'What did that contain?'

'How the hell should I know?' Paul Francis injected offence into his tone. 'I did the job for what it was worth, determined the root of title, checked the registry, and did a brief flip through the supporting papers. But I didn't read it all; hell, why should I? There were papers of instructions to the Jennings solicitors, by the man himself; there were papers dealt with by the executors of his will; the will was annexed and all that. But a lot of it was unnecessary to the conveyance itself, and there was no need. Anyway, if it's all so important, ask Sam Saxby for the files back.'

'No, it isn't important. And I presume Sam Saxby will have turned the papers over to his mother anyway.'

Paul Francis looked up at him defiantly. 'So that's it, then, is it? A visit and an interrogation for nothing. You're so bloody self-righteous, Eric, don't you know that? You never make a blasted mistake; you never step out of line; and you're always so ready to blast lesser mortals. I tell you straight, I was glad to get out of Francis, Shaw and Elder, and you were one of the bloody reasons why I was glad.'

Eric Ward stared at the barrister. For a moment he was surprised by the vehemence of the outburst,· and then he was puzzled. The sudden attack held a hint of relief; it was as though a burden had been lifted from Paul Francis and the freedom he suddenly felt had been an opening of floodgates, a release from tension. Slowly Eric said, 'Perhaps you're right, Paul. Maybe I am difficult to live with, in the firm.'

'Too damned right,' Paul Francis said maliciously. 'You ought to hear Joseph about it. Oh, don't get me wrong, my old man knows when to use someone like you, dredge every last bit of work out of you. Couldn't do it with me, so was pleased enough to see me do my own thing at the Bar. But you, oh, he's got your bloody measure. But it doesn't mean he likes your mealy mouth, and it doesn't mean he doesn't like to see you eat dirt once in a while, believe me!'

Eric Ward stared at him, thinking. Paul Francis's eyes were unnaturally bright, triumphant; but it was a triumph built on a shaky confidence, for even as Eric stared at him he saw the movement in the pale eyes, the shifting of vaguely seen anxieties. 'What is it, Paul?' he asked suddenly, and the movement in the barrister's eyes became a swift flicker of alarm.

'What do you mean?'

'No. What do *you* mean?' Eric insisted.'

'Suddenly you feel confident enough to bawl me out. Why?'

'A few home truths—'

'Or a satisfaction in getting off too lightly.' Eric paused, thinking back over the last few minutes and his conversation with the barrister. 'I get the feeling you haven't told me everything,' he said slowly.

'I've told you—'

'Or maybe I didn't ask the right questions,' Eric said.

The silence grew between them. Paul Francis was unable to meet his eyes as Eric waited, thinking. There was something he had missed; something Paul Francis had expected him to ask and was relieved that he had not.

Then Francis stood up, setting aside his glass. 'I've got a dinner appointment,' he lied. 'I think you'd better go now, Eric. I've nothing more to say.'

Eric rose, his eyes still fixed on the barrister and he noted the evasiveness of his eyes, the nervousness of his hands. He was right; there was something. Eric followed Paul Francis as he walked quickly to the door, stood there holding it open, waiting for Eric Ward to leave.

And then, slowly, the sections slipped into place, the unanswered question rose in his mind. In the doorway he turned, looked at the barrister silently for a moment.

'You drew up that option to purchase,' Eric said.

'I've already said so—'

'And failed to register it.'

'An oversight. Now look—'

The words died on his lips as Eric stared silently at him for several seconds. 'Amos Saxby and Ellen Saxby entered into a conveyance of Holton Hill Farm to defeat the unregistered option to purchase,' Eric said quietly. 'They didn't come to Francis, Shaw and Elder to do the conveyancing. They went to a Berwick firm, who had no previous knowledge of the issues. But Cranby never met Amos Saxby until he went to the Old Vicarage for *instructions.'*

'I don't see—'

'Amos already knew what instructions to give, because he and Ellen and maybe Sam too, they all knew what the effect of lack of registration of the option would be; they must have known, because that was the purpose of the conveyance to Amos.'

Paul Francis began to close the door. His face was pale. Eric put out a hand, holding the door open. 'Someone will have had to explain it to them; they will have had to receive legal advice, the kind that would warn them that Francis, Shaw and Elder would refuse to complete it because of prior knowledge, imputed knowledge, of the lack of registration. Who gave them that advice, Paul? Who did they go to, to get a legal viewpoint?'

Paul Francis's lips were as pale as his face; he stood framed in the doorway, the fear in his eyes now naked, and unhidden. 'You unethical bastard,' Eric Ward said.

* * *

The more he thought about it, the more angry Eric Ward became. Paul Francis's conduct had been reprehensible on two counts. The first was that having displayed his incompetence by failing to register the option to purchase, he had then compounded that sin by advising the Saxbys of the effects of that failure. There was no doubt he had, by some form of twisted logic, absolved himself of guilt in the matter by arguing that since he was no longer with Francis, Shaw and Elder there was nothing legally or morally wrong in advising Amos Saxby of his failure to complete the requisite formalities, and the consequent effects, but it was a logic Eric was entirely unable to accept. But the second ground for criticism of Paul Francis was the professional one. It was clear that when Amos Saxby took advice from Paul Francis it had been a situation where client was consulting barrister direct. No reputable solicitor would have put a brief of that kind to a member of the Bar — and barristers were not allowed, as a matter of professional ethics, to deal direct with clients. That was the privilege of the solicitor. Eric was severely tempted to report Paul Francis to the Bar Council and his temper grew worse, because he knew that he would not do so — whatever Paul's failings, he was just starting to make a successful career free from the shadow of his father and Eric Ward could not do it to the man, however contemptible his conduct might have been.

But that left Eric with a further problem. Within the hour, Sandra Saxby would be calling upon him, at his request. The information he now held was dangerous; if he released it, she might use it against Paul Francis. He guessed she would be vindictive enough. On the other hand, if he withheld the information from her it could be argued he was compounding Paul Francis's professional crime, to the detriment of his client. It was a nice point.

And in the tangled tensions of the Saxby family, he could not even be sure that she did not already know of the situation in which Paul Francis had got caught up. At the earliest moment he would have to tell Joseph —and leave it to the father to sort out why on earth the son must have behaved the way he did. Eric himself had only one conclusion to draw: struggling in his early weeks at the Bar, Paul had grabbed at the chance of a fat, undeclared fee from Amos Saxby — for there could be no doubt Amos would have been prepared to pay handsomely for information that would scotch the hopes of his youngest son. Though why he should want to do so remained a mystery to Eric.

There was a tap on the door and Philippa entered. 'Mr Ward?'

'Yes?'

'Mrs Saxby is here. I've asked her to wait a few minutes. I thought you might wish to make a call first.'

She had an oddly prim smirk on her lips. 'Call?' he asked, puzzled.

'A Miss Morcomb. She called two days ago; again yesterday. She left this number when she rang today.'

Philippa handed him a slip of paper. He stared at it, aware of the slow flush that was staining his face; aware also of the dull ache of longing that moved through his body. 'Thank you, Philippa. You can send Mrs Saxby in.'

'But aren't you—'

'Send her in.'

She raised her eyebrows, turned, and headed for the door. He called her name. When she turned, expectantly, with the smile beginning to return he had pleasure in saying, 'And I'd like you to get in touch with the Public Record Office. As quickly as possible, I want a copy of the will of Frank Jennings. He died about 1967.'

It was the one document that would be on file, for certain, and it might throw some light upon the Holton Hill Farm issue as a whole.

'Certainly, Mr Ward. Oh, and it's Mrs and *Mr* Saxby who's waiting.'

'*Mr* Saxby?'

It was Colin Saxby.

He came in behind his sister-in-law, diffidently, a hint of reluctance in his gait. He glanced briefly at Eric and shook hands but did not take the proffered seat; instead, he went to stand uneasily beside the window, part of the proceedings, yet distant from them. Sandra Saxby, on the other hand, was completely at ease and more; there was an air of confidence about her, some of the lines of dissatisfaction had smoothed from around her mouth and Eric suspected that the dark clothes she wore were more a sop to convention than a sign of conviction. She may well have grieved and be in mourning for her dead husband, but either she dissembled well or Eric was doing her a severe injustice. She appeared to him relaxed, and in control of a situation she had previously found annoying, distasteful and hateful.

Somehow, and the word came unbidden to him she seemed fulfilled.

She sat down and smiled faintly. 'I hope you didn't mind Colin coming along. I asked him to ... to look after my interests. We ... we are old friends.'

'And now brother and sister-in-law,' Eric added, and had the vague satisfaction of seeing Colin Saxby move and shuffle uneasily near the window.

'You asked me to call,' Sandra Saxby said and her tone was cooler.

'I thought we'd better have a chat.'

'About what's to be done now?' She gave Eric a look that could be described only as smouldering. 'Jack's dead, but that changes nothing. He intended to get his rights. I still intend to do just that.'

'Yes well—'

'You advised that a suit against the executors — the bank that acted for Mrs Ellen Saxby — would be advisable. I don't see there's any problem. Presumably, as Jack's widow, I can simply carry on the fight. The ... cause of action, you call it? It doesn't end with Jack's death, does it?'

Eric shook his head. 'No, it doesn't. You're quite right in your assessment. But—'

'Then we'll continue the fight,' she interrupted firmly.

Colin Saxby moved uncomfortably behind her. 'Sandra, I think you'd better slow down ... listen to Mr Ward.'

For a moment Eric thought she was going to rebel but the quick movement of her head subsided and she stared at Eric sombrely. 'All right — what do you want to say?'

'It's really to discuss the wisdom of continuing with the suit at this point.'

'You agreed the cause of action does not die—'

'Please, hear me out.' Eric waited until the battle glint faded in the formidable eyes of Mrs Saxby. 'While your husband was alive I was in favour of the action. There was every reason to get an order for specific performance — the farm was his on lease, he wanted to farm it. But now ... would *you* want to farm it?'

Her eyes were chilly and her jaw suddenly fierce. 'No — but there's the matter of my child to consider.'

'Child?'

She smiled grimly. 'I'm pregnant. Jack will have a posthumous child. And if I can get the farm from that crazy old man I can sell it, and provide for Jack's child. So nothing has changed, you understand?'

'There's every chance Amos Saxby will fight,' Eric said doubtfully. 'You might, if you win, get costs against him. Either way you won't get back what is spent in lawyers' fees—'

'Ha!' She glared at him suspiciously. 'An honest lawyer?'

Eric ignored the gibe. Patiently, he went on: 'There's little point in incurring the expense of trial if it's not necessary. There are other ways of skinning the cat ... and less expensive ones.'

'I'm all ears,' Sandra Saxby said contemptuously.

'It's quite simple,' Eric said. 'Let me talk to Amos Saxby again.'

A slow stain of anger marked her fair skin. 'Fat lot of good that will do!'

'I'm not so sure.' Eric glanced briefly at the silent Colin Saxby and then went on: 'He was very upset at his wife's death; he said silly things in court. But now, with Jack dead, maybe he's had time to think things through. I think maybe part of the attitude he adopted earlier was the need to humiliate your husband, show him up, *beat* him in this issue. That chance is gone now; maybe he'll be more inclined to listen to reason.'

She hesitated, uncertain. Colin Saxby moved behind her, leaned forward. 'Might be worth a go, Sandy.'

She did not look at him, but kept her eyes fixed on Eric Ward. 'How would you approach him?'

'Using the same argument I have with you. He can't *want* litigation. The case, if it comes on, will cause quite a stir: a family affair being dragged into the courts, with charges of breach of contract and conspiracy to defraud. He can't want the experience; he'd certainly not enjoy it, particularly if he lost.'

'And we *can* win, can't we?' she said sharply.

Eric raised a warning hand. 'These things are never watertight — and we've not got all the ammunition we need.'

'Such as?'

'The reason why Amos was so keen to stop Jack getting the farm.'

Her eyes became vague, almost glassy; her lips were set in a thin line. She shook her head. When she spoke, her tone was bitter. 'He always hated me; me and my father. He thought I wasn't good enough for his precious sons. He almost destroyed my life once ...' There was an involuntary jerk of her head as she caught herself in time, stopped herself from casting a furious glance at Colin Saxby. 'And when I was married to Jack he was barely civil to us, all over the years. But even then I didn't realize how really vindictive he was. Those years we farmed Holton Hill — he let us believe we'd own the farm one day soon. The option to purchase ... he never said a word at the time. But he was plotting, you see? He had a grand strategy. You know what he's like; you know the theatrical way he behaves. That would have been his intention, if we hadn't forced the issue; if Colin hadn't told us that the silly old woman had conveyed the farm to Amos! It would have come as a great shock, you see: Amos would have waited for the best time, the most crushing time to let that cat out of the bag! He'd have let us go on in our ignorance, let us break our backs, build up the farm and our hopes, and then one day, when we were at our most vulnerable, he would have crushed us with the information. That *he* owned Holton Hill Farm; that the option to purchase was worthless! Can't you see how deeply he hates me? To do that kind of thing to us? And can't you see how much I'm determined never to let him get away with it?'

Her voice had streaks of hysteria threading through it, and her face was red with anger. She caught at a stray lock of her black hair and thrust it away from her eyes in a violent gesture, while, placatingly, Colin Saxby moved forward, put a soothing hand on her shoulder. Then, perhaps conscious of Eric's gaze, he removed his hand, and went back to stand by the window again.

A short silence fell. Eric leaned back in his chair uneasily. He was convinced of her hatred, but not by her explanation of Amos's motivation. She was an egocentric woman who saw, in her domination of her dead husband, a role that would inevitably have raised Amos Saxby's ire: she had almost taken one son, and had succeeded in taking the other. It was *possible* she was right, but Eric suspected it was not the complete story. The reaction of Ellen and Amos Saxby to the option to purchase had come too swiftly; besides, if Amos really felt the way she suggested, he would never have agreed to his wife making the option in the first place. There was something missing in her thesis. But it made no difference, essentially.

'Well, what am I to do, Mrs Saxby? My advice is, let me make another attempt ... try to get Amos Saxby to see reason. Do you agree to this?'

She hesitated. Her voice was softer as she half turned in the chair. 'Colin?'

'I think Mr Ward is right. Let him have another go. In any case, there's nothing to be lost, is there?'

Eric nodded. 'If my attempt fails, you can still proceed to action.'

She stood up, taking a decision with what he suspected would be typical swiftness. 'Then it's agreed. You'll let me know, Mr Ward?'

'As soon as I can.'

She turned to Colin. 'You said in about half an hour's time?'

'I'll meet you at the restaurant, Sandy.' he said. 'If I can just have a few words with Mr Ward.'

She smiled, nodded to Eric briefly and marched from the room, slender, willowy, but as tough a widow as Eric had ever come across. When the door closed behind her he turned to Colin Saxby. 'You wanted to discuss something? Take a seat.'

Colin Saxby pulled a face and sat down.

He seemed thinner in his features than previously, and there were dark shadows under his eyes. Eric suspected he might be taking the loss of his brother more severely than Sandra was taking the loss of her husband. He certainly seemed to be suffering from a degree of strain; but then, again, it might have been due to finding that emotional ties he had once had with Sandra King could become trammelling again, but this time with his pregnant sister-in-law. Eric remembered the soothing hand on her shoulder and he wondered — he could imagine what Detective-Superintendent Freddie Jenkins might have made of it.

'What can I do for you?' he asked.

Colin Saxby shrugged. 'I just thought ... I'd better be here with Sandra ... she can get a bit excited, say things she doesn't mean ...'

'I'm sure she appreciated your company.' Eric said drily. 'As she and her husband will have appreciated your telling them about the conveyance to defeat their option in the first instance. How ... er ... how did you come to find out about it?'

For a moment Colin Saxby looked startled. His eyes were suddenly evasive, and anxious. 'I ... er ... I just found out. Mother ... I was looking through some papers, and Mother ... Anyway, I had a row with Amos, and after that I thought it my duty to tell Jack.'

Duty, Eric Ward thought; as he looked at Colin Saxby, he could believe the man would have accepted the concept of duty in the Army, but to his brother? When he had accepted no ties of duty to Sandra King, deserting her in face of Amos

Saxby's wrath, or to his father, when he sold Brookfield Farm after his father gave it to him for a song? The word did not fall easily from Colin Saxby's lips.

'Were you and Jack very close?' Eric asked.

Colin Saxby smiled thinly. 'All three of us tended to go our own ways. But I didn't really come here to talk about the past, or about Holton Hill Farm. It's about the other night, really.'

'At Stoneleigh's party?'

Saxby nodded. He looked slyly at Eric Ward. 'I got pretty drunk.'

'You did.'

'And amorous.'

'I—'

'And unsuccessfully so. No matter about that; if she wanted to go with Stoneleigh, that' was up to her. No ...' He hesitated. 'I have a vague recollection of talking to you as I was leaving the club.'

'You did speak to us, yes.'

'What did I say?' The words rushed out, as though Eric's answer was important and eagerly awaited. Eric was nonplussed. He could hardly remember the conversation. He told Saxby so.

'But what did I talk *about?*'

'I really can't recall. There were some general remarks about Jack and your father. I think you expressed the opinion that neither of them could win, in the end. I was rather inclined to agree with you, as a matter of fact, Mr Saxby.'

'And I said ... nothing more?' When Eric shook his head a certain relief seemed to touch Saxby's anxious mouth. Then he darted another quick glance at Eric. 'I ... I didn't have my keys in my hand, did I?'

'Not that I saw.'

'Sam's car, you see. Someone stole it. I wasn't too happy at having to tell him, I can tell you. And then I couldn't even find him. Wandered around till three in the bloody morning.' He shook his head. 'And then there was Jack ...

They told us down at the station, next day. Bad business, hit-and-run. Bad business ...'

He fidgeted in his seat, uncertain. Eric watched him, silently, curious as to what had made Colin Saxby stay on after Sandra had left. His conversation at the club had been drunkenly innocuous, yet it seemed to have left the man nervous and edgy. Or was it an excuse, to raise some other issue?

'Think ... I think I saw you talking with Cranston at one point, didn't I?' It had been a struggle to get the question out.

'Sir John Freshfield's financial adviser? Yes, we had a sort of social chat.'

'Did he ... er ... did he say anything about the Stoneleigh Project?' Colin Saxby licked his lips. 'I can ask you, since you're linked with Stoneleigh, aren't you?'

'The firm acts for him ... or will do so,' Eric agreed. 'But I'm not sure—'

'Did he say Freshfield would give it backing?'

Eric hesitated, not sure he should repeat Cranston's conversation. Then he took pity on the sweating Colin Saxby. 'He ... was not impressed by the venture. If you want my advice, it would be worth looking elsewhere for financial support.'

Colin Saxby stared at him. The corners of his mouth were white. 'Is ... is that what he said?'

'More or less.'

'Damn it—'

The phone rang. Eric picked it up and Philippa told him there was a call for him. For a moment Eric thought it might be Anne Morcomb and he did not want to speak to her yet, not until he had sorted out his mind and his emotions. 'Who is it?' he asked.

'Detective-Superintendent Jenkins.'

'All right, put him through.'

The cheery tones of the Welsh police officer came through almost immediately. 'Hello, old son. Just been along to get a report from the forensic labs at Gosforth. Knew you'd be fascinated to hear the result ...'

As the detective-superintendent talked Eric watched Colin Saxby. The man was sitting back in his chair, seemingly drained of energy; his eyes were vacant, his mouth slack, but his fingers were making small jerking movements on the arm of the chair, indicative of a nervous tension that must be gripping him, causing his blood to flow hot and fast and fearful.

When the call was over, Eric put down the phone and looked at Saxby. 'Are you all right?'

Life returned to the vacant eyes. Colin Saxby sat up, nodding. 'Yes, certainly. Sorry about that. Er ... well, there's nothing more I wanted to say, really. Just a chat. But ... well, there is one thing.'

'Yes?'

'The ... er ... thing about my telling Jack and Sandra about the conveyance. You see, it was all Amos's doing, really. Mother didn't want to do it — she was distressed. She told me about it and as I said, I thought it my duty.' His eyes met Eric's briefly.

'If it was Amos's idea and your mother was unhappy, why did she go through with the conveyance?' Eric asked. 'Why exactly was Amos suddenly so bitter towards Jack?'

'That's difficult to explain,' Saxby said hurriedly. 'It's family business. Even Sandra doesn't know ... But look, the thing I wanted to say was about my telling Jack. You see, Amos doesn't know I was the one who told him. And ... well, I wouldn't want him to know, you understand.' His eyes were almost pleading. 'It's particularly important, just at this time.'

'He'll not hear it from me, Mr Saxby.' Colin Saxby's gratitude showed in his face. He rose, thanked Eric and turned to head for the door. Eric stopped him.

'Mr Saxby, I think you'd better know.'

'Yes?'

'That was Detective-Superintendent Jenkins on the phone. He's just had the results of some forensic tests. They are largely scrapings of paint, hair and blood from the motor vehicle that killed your brother Jack. They found the car, abandoned, in a hut on some waste ground in Byker. They did the tests straight away; they can prove it was the car that ran him down.'

Colin Saxby retraced his steps, gripped the back of the chair and stared at Eric Ward. He tried to speak, but no words came.

'The car,' Eric said gently, 'belongs to your brother Sam.'

The knuckles that lay on the chair-back turned white.

CHAPTER 5

Joseph Francis was not pleased. He said nothing to Eric Ward but each time they passed in the office his brow was thunderous and his glance coldly evasive. Eric could not be sure of the reason: he suspected that although the senior partner was not happy about the visit of Chief Superintendent Jenkins and the consequent information regarding the death of Jack Saxby, it was more likely that his displeasure was occasioned by a conversation with his son Paul. It was unlikely that Paul would have repeated the details of the discussion he had had with Eric, but enough would have been said to tell Joseph Francis that pressure had been brought upon his barrister son by Joseph's junior partner.

Whatever the reason might be, it soured the atmosphere in the office and the other people at Francis, Shaw and Elder were affected. There was a general edge to the conversation, a snappiness in replies, an overall impatience with mistakes and, inevitably in such a situation, the mistakes began to multiply.

It was a relief when the weekend arrived. The weather prospects were good so Eric decided to drive into Northumberland on the Sunday morning, go walking in the Cheviots, get some fresh air into his lungs. The intentions were, he believed, sincere and untrammelled, and yet when he drove past Wooler he found himself almost automatically taking the road out towards the Morcomb estates.

When he saw the sign pointing to Sedleigh Hall he hesitated, but then wrenched the wheel around, a sudden indecision seizing him. Then he drove on, following the line of the stream, winding his way through the narrow lanes, past the open fields and the tiny farms, until the car was running down the hill, through the scattering of houses flanking the Norman church at the centre of Seddon Burn.

And in a little while he came to the old, moss-grown ruins of the hall, still commanding its rolling aspect over the southerly hills, still approached by the thickly growing rhododendrons, and still forcing an abandonment of the car to walk the last three hundred yards through the tangle out of which loomed the disease-destroyed elms. And he was standing beside the fire-stricken walls of the old house, carpeted now by ivy and moss, and he could remember the first time he had come here.

He sat down and he waited, his eyes half closed against the brightness of the sun. An hour later, she came.

He heard the soft thudding of the horse's hooves on the turf and he turned his head, watching Anne Morcomb as she rode up towards him, her red-gold hair flaring in the sun. He had seen her like this before, on the black mare: this time it was different because almost three years had gone by and things had changed, become more defined, and more dangerous.

She drew in some short distance from him and sat still on the snorting animal, watching him silently. 'I saw your car,' she said at last. 'From the hill.'

He smiled wryly. 'And I ... I suppose I knew you were likely to stick to habits, and ride on a fine Sunday morning where you've ridden for years.'

She glanced past him at the ruins of Seddon Burn Hall. She grimaced. 'At least, you seem to remember. Even if you do refuse to answer my phone-calls.'

'I've been busy,' he said lamely, and as he saw her face tighten, he added, 'I'm sorry, that was stupid, a stupid thing to say. It's just that ... I needed time to think, and—'

'You make it all sound so *serious,*' she mocked him. 'I don't recall anything being said. And if you're concerned about words like seduction, well, as I recall, it was I who seduced you, if at all. You were a somewhat reluctant swain.'

He knew her well enough to be aware of the undercurrent of hurt in her voice, in spite of the mockery. It would perhaps be better to adopt the same pose, but it was important to him — that she understood. Yet he found it difficult to find the words. 'The reluctance ... it's not what you think.'

'No? You walked away once before; this was no surprise, though I thought—' She bit back the words; some of the tension in her must have been communicated to her mount, for the animal snorted, backed away, tossing its head. Eric watched her as she brought the mare under control.

'I should never have stayed,' he said levelly.

The remark brought her head up, angrily. 'What the hell are you talking about? What's the matter with you, Eric? I said before, I expected no promises from you, no cataclysmic decisions simply because we made love. But I did expect something more than mere silence: that was just an insult. I'm not asking, demanding anything of you — I never did. But why can't you just behave normally, relax, be yourself with me, instead of this screwed-up, tight, suspicious man who seems to be afraid to open his mouth unless his feelings run away with him?'

She didn't understand; she could not understand. She was too young. He could have told her of the pain and the anxiety, the dark uncertainties and the struggle of pride with despair. The bleakness of his future lay between them; the fact that she had the power to save him was no solution because the solution had to be one he forged for himself. But there was no way he could explain that to her, and it was better that no explanation was forthcoming at all.

'You're a fool, Eric Ward.' He made no reply, and suddenly, she smiled, not happily, but with a certain measure of understanding. 'You know what's worse? You're a fool who's fooling himself. You think you're doing the right thing, the noble thing — but there's no nobility in denial and folly. A couple of years ago I wanted to ask you something and you scuttled for cover for reasons I couldn't understand. Maybe I do understand now, though I can't accept the reasons. If there was anything real between us, the reasons would fall into place, become unimportant. And *I* think there is something sound between us ... for that reason I won't take silence for an answer. So, for whatever purpose you came out here, today isn't going to be the time to discuss it. This time, *I'm* leaving.'

She grinned at him, somewhat lopsidedly, and he thought he caught the glitter of tears in her eyes. He wanted to call out after her as she turned aside and rode back across the meadow, but his mouth was dry, and the thudding in his chest was almost painful. He cursed under his breath as she disappeared through the trees: why should he be damned with pride and age and illness when deep down he knew exactly what he wanted?

* * *

On the Monday morning, in the office, he was still racked with the same self-doubts. He attended to his tasks automatically, settling for straightforward drudgery, the completion of some conveyances, the settling of some accounts, the mathematical tasks of taxation settlements. He hardly touched his post, brought in by Philippa with his coffee, and it was almost midday before he saw that among the post was a registered envelope from London.

He slit open the envelope. Inside was a copy of the last will and testament of Francis Edward Jennings.

The telephone on his desk buzzed: it was reception. 'Mr Ward, there's a gentleman here to see you. A Mr ... er ... Parton?'

'Send him up.'

The ex-jockey slipped into the office two minutes later. He was wearing a check suit that would no doubt have caused considerable comment in the reception area downstairs and a lopsided grin that would equally have endeared him to the receptionist. Neither would have found favour with Joseph Francis had he come in at that moment, the more so as Jackie Parton drew forward a chair, sat down and put his feet on Eric Ward's desk. He grinned cheekily, his scarred lip lifting at the corner.

'So how's my favourite solicitor?'

Eric Ward grimaced. 'Not too enamoured of life right now. You heard the news about the car that killed Jack Saxby, at the Quayside?'

Jackie Parton nodded, took out a toothpick from his jacket pocket and began to tease at one of his front teeth. 'I heard. There's a fair bit of chat about Byker and Walker. The police have come heavy on some of the local tearaways, but there's no finger pointing at anyone. And the car belonged to Mr Samuel Saxby, hey?'

'That's about the size of it.'

'Hmmm. And what's his story, then?'

Eric shook his head. 'It wasn't he who had the car that evening. It was Colin Saxby.'

'And Colin Saxby?'

'Is scared as hell.' Eric paused. 'He's been in to see me. Someone stole the car, but it's all a bit odd. He and Samuel Saxby were wandering around Newcastle that night, the old man was on his way back from Sunderland ... but I've got the feeling there's some kind of undercurrent, some kind of tension among the group of them that I haven't been able to discover yet. I'm hoping you've come up with something.'

Jackie Parton inspected the toothpick. He shook his head doubtfully. 'Going to disappoint you,' he said. 'There's no whispers I can pick up.'

'Nothing at all?'

The ex-jockey caught the disappointment in Eric's tone and shrugged defensively. 'I tell you, I've done all the digging I could. I've done the rounds, talked to everyone who might come up with something. But farmers ... I tell you, Eric, they're a close-mouthed lot. They keep themselves to themselves. Life in these villages, on these farms, it tends to be close. Oh, I got a couple of stories, you know: fact that there was a bit of trouble between Colin Saxby and his father, which ended with Colin charging off to join the Army—'

'That would have been over Sandra Saxby.'

'Right. And Sam Saxby, he has the reputation of being a bit of a money-grabber, you know? Keen to get his hands on a good thing. Burned his fingers a bit over some land purchases a few years ago at Berwick —' .

'When he employed the Berwick solicitors.'

'—and reputed to be keeping close to the old man to end up with the largest slice of the legacy cake when Amos pops off. Greedy so-and-so, is the talk.'

'And the warfare between Amos and Jack Saxby?'

Jackie Parton considered for a moment, then shook his head. 'Just seemed to spring up. The trial caused some local comment and speculation, but no one seems to have any idea why Ellen and Amos Saxby got sour on their youngest son.

'I'm not sure it was both of them. Colin Saxby sort of hinted that it was really Amos's doing; Jack's mother wasn't too happy about the whole thing.'

Jackie Parton stared at him for a moment. 'But it was her farm. She didn't *have* to make it over to Amos, and do down her youngest son. I gather he's a domineering old bastard, but, hell, if she was so upset, why did she do it?'

'You've not been able to find out?' Eric asked.

'Not a whisper. Whatever Jack did to upset the old man, it must have been very much a family matter. They've kept it very close. No gossip; no chat.'

It was frustrating. Eric Ward was not certain that the line of enquiry was even likely to be useful if it proved fruitful, but he now felt somehow involved in the affairs of the Saxby family. He had liked Jack Saxby, if not his wife, and he had wanted justice for him, a patent justice in a situation that was clearly one based on a family squabble. Amos Saxby's theatrical histrionics had not endeared him to Eric Ward, and the whole arrangement he had come to with his wife smacked of sharp practice. Ellen Saxby was dead and a secret might had died with her, for Eric doubted that Amos or his sons would now divulge reasons, with both Ellen and Jack dead.

'This ... er ... hit-and-run,' Jackie Parton was saying. 'If it was Sam Saxby's car, are the police pressurizing him, or Colin?'

'I don't know.'

'Would either have a motive for wanting to kill Jack Saxby?'

Eric thought back over the events of the last weeks. Colin Saxby could have no motive — and then Eric thought of the way in which Colin had come forward as Sandra Saxby's support. They had been lovers once: could it have been a strong enough passion to have withstood her marriage to Jack, and provided a motive for action? And Samuel Saxby — could he have seen the withering away of his father's money in pointless litigation as a reason for removing the cause of the litigation? Mentally, Eric discarded both suggestions on grounds of logic, yet a tiny voice insisted that murder was rarely based upon a logical view of a situation.

'I mean,' Jackie Parton was saying, 'Amos Saxby made his dislike clear enough to discount him, hey? Unless by *showing* his dislike he was making a double bluff. You know, make it so obvious that no one would suspect him of knocking off his son thereafter.'

Eric Ward waved his hand in a nervous, irritable gesture. 'Makes no difference, anyway, Jackie. I didn't really want you to start delving into this killing. It's all nothing to do with me: my instructions concern the resolution of this civil case, and my job now is to try to make Amos Saxby see sense, avoid litigation, settle out of court and pay Sandra Saxby the value of the land her husband would have got. I merely thought that if I could discover the reason for the family split, I might use it to lever the old man into a compromise. But if you say there's no information ...'

'None at all.' Jackie Parton inspected his toothpick again, then dropped it, somewhat chewed, into the ashtray on Eric's desk. 'The only bit of information I *have* come up with is on the way they've been investing their money. I don't suppose it's important, but I'd had a chat with some people I know in the broking business and they told me a few things.'

'Stockbrokers! I didn't know you moved in that kind of circle, Jackie!'

Jackie Parton grinned. 'Gambling is gambling, friend. The stock market, dogs, horses ... you'd be surprised how much they overlap, in the punting sense.'

'And the Saxbys have been playing the market?'

The ex-jockey shook his head. 'No, that isn't the message. You heard of this firm Stoneleigh Enterprises?'

Eric looked up in surprise. 'Yes, of course, we'll be doing some work for them if they ever really get off the ground.'

'Well, if they do get off the ground, it'll be on Saxby money to a fair amount.'

Eric frowned. 'How do you mean?'

'Colin Saxby's in for a fair bit. Sold his farm and ploughed most of his ready cash into the enterprise, I'm told.'

'I knew he'd put some in—'

'Almost all, is my information,' Jackie Parton interrupted. 'But apparently old Amos is in for a fair whack too. So I'm told.'

Eric found the information surprising. Amos Saxby's contact with the Honourable Antony Stoneleigh had not come to light previously; nothing of his involvement appeared in the files held by Francis, Shaw and Elder, and although Colin Saxby clearly was personally interested in the fortunes of the Stoneleigh project, he was a different proposition from his father.' And Amos Saxby's situation was different too: a retired man, he would be unwise to be gambling in such a project. 'You say Amos is in for a fair whack?'

'Well,' Jackie Parton conceded, 'the information's a bit vague. Colin Saxby has put in cash; the old man, well, it might be some kind of option or guarantee or something. I don't understand too much about this kind of thing, you know; the horses, yes, but shares ... they're beyond me. What I've been told is that this Stoneleigh feller has been trying to raise cash from the merchant banks—'

'That's right. It was the reason for the party for Sir John Freshfield.'

'A sweetener, hey?' Jackie Parton grinned.

'Which isn't going to work, apparently. But Amos-?'

'It seems he's backing the project in some way. His name has certainly been used in the bid to raise cash with the banks, but the extent of his involvement, I'm not sure about that.'

Eric Ward shook his head. 'All I can say is, both he and Colin Saxby are likely to catch a financial cold over that one, if Sir John Freshfield's financial adviser has any say in the matter.'

It was something that niggled away at the back of his mind after the ex-jockey had gone. Eric found it puzzling that Amos Saxby's involvement with Stoneleigh Enterprises had been so vaguely worded by Jackie Parton, and did not appear in the files held in the office. But then he shrugged it aside and picked up the document received from Public Records.

It was straightforward enough in its terms. Frank Jennings had been comfortably off, owning two farms. One he had left to a younger brother. The second — Holton Hill Farm — had been the subject of a legacy to Ellen Saxby, his second cousin. Frank Jennings had been predeceased by his wife, and there had been no children of the marriage. It gave no clue to what might have caused the rift between Amos and Jack Saxby. Eric Ward put the will aside and returned to other work in hand. He was half way through drafting a brief to counsel when his mind began to stray. He sat for a little while, thinking, and then he returned to the will on his desk. He read aloud the clause relating to the Ellen Saxby legacy.

'And to my cousin Ellen Saxby, of Eastgate Farm, Northumberland, in consideration of love and affection and knowing that she will carry out my wishes in the matter, I leave in fee simple the property known as Holton Hill Farm, without encumbrances of any kind whatsoever ...'

He stared at it for several minutes, thinking hard. There was something there, something odd. He dredged back in his mind, then rose, walked across to the bookshelves and considered the matter. He stared vacantly at the blue and gold spines, hardly seeing them, as the words and phrases and consequences ticked over in his brain. Then, seeking confirmation of the burgeoning doubts in his mind, he reached out for one volume and ran his finger down the index. Within seconds he found what he wanted; a quick check of the relevant page and he obtained the confirmation he was seeking.

He went back to his desk, sat down, and re-read the will. There was nothing else there; no hint. No codicil, no attached papers. He picked up the phone.

'Philippa? I'll be out of the office this afternoon. If I'm required, I'll be at the Old Vicarage in Morpeth. That's right ... Amos Saxby's home.'

* * *

The grey stone and slate of the Old Vicarage seemed gloomy and forbidding under the mantle of light rain that had greeted Eric as he drove into Morpeth. He could not see the surrounding hills and the trees in the orchard dripped miserably as he parked the car in the driveway and walked towards the heavy front door. He rang the bell and above his head the stained-glass window seemed dulled and colourless. The house was silent.

Eric rang again and after a few seconds heard someone approaching the door. When it opened Eric found himself face to face once again with the tall, pale-eyed, sandy-haired figure of Samuel Saxby.

'Mr Ward.'

'I was hoping to see Amos Saxby for a few moments,' Eric said stiffly. 'Is he at home?'

Samuel Saxby's pale eyes flickered about as though seeking escape. He hesitated, glanced at his watch as though it played some part in his decision and then nodded, somewhat reluctantly. 'He's home ... but I'm not sure ...'

'It's quite important.'

'Yes.' Sam Saxby considered further, his glance sweeping across the drive to the roadway. 'He is ... expecting some visitors, so he won't be able to give you much time.'

'It shouldn't take long,' Eric announced crisply and moved inside the doorway. The rain was beginning to drip inside his coat collar. Sam Saxby stepped back, still reluctant, and then turned and headed towards the sitting-room where Amos Saxby had previously received Eric Ward. 'My father's in the bathroom,' Sam Saxby explained. 'He'll be down in a moment. You can wait here.'

Once again he consulted his watch. Eric ran a tentative finger inside his damp collar and then glanced curiously at Sam Saxby. 'You seem to spend a lot of time here at the Vicarage.'

'Not really,' Sam Saxby replied quickly. 'I call a couple of times each week, to see how Amos is. You just happened to have called while I'm here.'

'How is he taking the loss of his wife ... and son?' Eric asked.

The pale eyes regarded him dispassionately, giving nothing away. 'Amos is a very strong and determined man. He lets nothing ... not even personal loss ... stand in his way. You will discover that. I presume you *have* come to talk about the suit?'

'Something like that,' Eric conceded. He looked directly at Sam Saxby. 'Talking of loss, have the police returned your car yet?'

For a long moment Sam Saxby was silent. He turned away and walked towards the window, looked out over the sad, dripping garden. 'They still have it. Tests, they say. In due course, I understand, they'll return it.'

'And still no idea who took it?' Eric persisted.

'I have no idea.' Sam Saxby turned to face Eric. 'Whether *they* do or not, I can't say. They haven't confided in me.'

'Odd coincidence, though. I mean, that it was your car that killed your brother.'

Samuel Saxby was very much in control of his feelings. He betrayed them by not a single flicker of his eyelids; there was the steel of his father in him, if not his father's theatricality. 'They questioned me about the ... accident. I couldn't help them. Colin—' he could not disguise the hint of contempt that crept in his tone — 'Colin was too drunk to know what was going on at the time, and he can't even be sure what time he parked the car, or even where, with precision.'

'And the car keys?'

The pale eyes regarded Eric coldly. 'Have not been found.' He hesitated. 'I understand you were at the same ... party as Colin.'

'That's right. But I haven't been able to help the police much, either.' Eric eyed Samuel Saxby carefully, not certain whether to proceed. 'I ... er ... I had a chat with Paul Francis the other day.'

Sam Saxby wrinkled his brow in mock concentration, pretending to have to think about the name. 'Paul Francis ... the barrister?'

'That's him. He did some work for you, when you had the wayleave trouble over Eastgate Farm.'

'I do recall,' Sam Saxby said drily, but his tongue came out, flicking nervously over his lips.

'He told me some interesting things,' Eric remarked quietly.

'Such as?'

'Such as you may well have held on to files belonging to Francis, Shaw and Elder.'

The silence grew around them, lengthened, became tense. Sam Saxby stood woodenly, expressionless, a man in external control of himself but one nevertheless who would be seething with questions inside. He made a deprecating gesture with his left hand. 'I ... I think you've been misinformed.'

'He came out to discuss wayleave matters and brief to counsel. He brought appropriate files with him, relating to Saxby transactions. As far as he can recall, he didn't take those files away with him.'

Sam Saxby managed a thin smile; it gave the appearance of a confidence Eric suspected he did not feel. 'If that were so, it doesn't matter, surely? If such files related to Saxby transactions, the papers in them would belong by right to the family, and the solicitors would have no legal right to their retention anyway.'

Eric Ward stared at him challengingly. 'That presupposes the material in the files went to the people they concerned,' he said.

'But they did, young man, they did!' the voice boomed from behind him. Eric turned and Amos Saxby made his entrance.

He was dressed in a lounge suit and wore a carnation in his lapel. His hair had been recently brushed, and his blue, ice-cold eyes were sparkling, clearly enjoying the situation. There was some kind of subdued excitement in his bearing and Eric wondered how much of the conversation the old man had heard: he gained the impression that Amos Saxby was enjoying the pressure Eric had been putting on his son, and had been waiting in the corridor outside the room choosing the most appropriate moment to make his entry upon the scene. Now he strode across the room and stood with his back to the Adam fireplace, arms folded across his chest. He smiled with a grim confidence at Eric Ward.

'The files I'm talking about,' Eric said, 'concerned Holton Hill Farm.'

136

'They went to my wife,' Amos Saxby said, 'and that's that, isn't it?'

Stiffly, Eric began, 'If that can be proved—'

'Doesn't have to be proved,' Amos Saxby boomed enjoyably. 'Family files; came to the family; *you* prove something out of it. I don't have to. Now then, let's get on with this. Sam let you in so I suppose you have something to say to me. Get on and say it; I have some business to attend to shortly, and am expecting some visitors, so, keep it short, young man. And sweet.'

Sam Saxby stepped back, away from his father and stood near the window in an almost unconscious gesture of subservience. Eric glanced at him curiously: Jackie Parton had said Sam Saxby had a reputation for greed. Was it the hope of succession to his father's money that made him take this role? Eric turned back to the old man. 'I've come on behalf of Mrs Sandra Saxby.'

'That bitch,' the old man said warmly. 'Of course you have. And what does she want to do? Give up the fight?'

'Your son is dead, Mr Saxby.'

Amos Saxby's cold eyes glittered. 'I know It. So ...?'

'So is there any point in continuing this fight? Whatever caused the rift between you and your son, doesn't it end with his death? What's to be gained by further litigation? Why not reach an accommodation with your son's widow? You surely can't think—'

'What do *you* think, Sam?'

Sam Saxby jerked at the sudden question. He looked at Eric, then his father. He shrugged, lamely. 'It's not my business. Holton Hill Farm—'

'Could be yours, in time,' the old man interrupted. There was irony in his tone when he went on. 'You must have *some* interest in its disposition.'

Sam Saxby licked his lips. He locked his hands behind his back, and rocked nervously on his heels. 'I ... I think we ought to hear what Mr Ward proposes,' he suggested. 'On Sandra's behalf.'

'That's it.' Amos Saxby breathed heavily through his nostrils, a charger about to enter battle. 'Let's hear it then, Sandra Saxby's proposals.'

Eric nodded. 'They are quite simple. She doesn't want a protracted legal battle. She doesn't want the family name dragged through the courts—'

'Ha!'

'She doesn't see the point of further expense, which might drain away family assets, when the matter might be settled amicably—'

'Amicably?'

'So she proposes, without prejudice,' Eric continued calmly, 'a settlement out of court.'

'No doubt, no doubt,' Amos Saxby said grimly. 'And such a settlement would comprise?'

Eric paused, glanced at them in turn: they both had something to gain or lose in this situation. 'I am instructed that Mrs Sandra Saxby would be prepared to relinquish her claim to Holton Hill Farm, and bring to an end the present proceedings against you in return for the price of the land and buildings, at valuation, and her expenses, suitably taxed, to date.'

Amos Saxby glared at him; his hands were clenched at his side and he gave every appearance of a man bursting with rage except that his blue eyes remained ice-cold, calm, calculating. 'She doesn't want much! The price of the farm, plus *expenses,* when she's got no right to the damn place!'

'The conveyance—'

'Was legal! Ellen made the farm over to me and that was the end of that! And you can tell your blasted client that there is no power on earth that will make me reach a settlement with her! She doesn't stand a cat in hell's chance in this case, and you know it, so you come crawling along here trying to outwit an old man! It won't happen, my friend; there'll be no compromise. I wouldn't give that cat a penny of mine: she came from a no-good family and she's no good herself. She thought she could bed down into this family when she carried on with Colin: I stopped that. She succeeded with

138

Jack — he was too damned stubborn to listen to me. Well, hard luck — there's no way she's going to win through in the end when her husband's dead!'

'Mr Saxby, irrespective of your feelings for Mrs Saxby, I think—'

'I don't give a damn what you think! And let's not get the wrong idea. I hate that cat, but it would have been the same even if Jack had still been alive! The farm is mine; Jack would never have got it, and I'm damned sure she won't get it — or its price!'

'Then you won't agree to a settlement?'

'Dad—' Sam Saxby said warningly, to Eric's surprise. Amos Saxby thrust the restraint aside.

'Stuff your settlement! And you can get out now. I've got business matters to discuss.'

'Not yet,' Eric said evenly. He was becoming irritated by the old man's hectoring manner, and there were hints of pain behind his eyes. Deliberately, avoiding the trap of stress and tension that he suspected the old man was leading him into, he said, 'We have one further matter to discuss.'

The ice-blue eyes gleamed, the glance sharpening as a hint of real, rather than simulated anger moved into Amos Saxby's voice. 'I told you our talk is over. This is my house. I want you out.'

'Not until we've first of all discussed Frank Jennings's will.'

For the first time Eric noticed the ticking of the clock on the mantelpiece behind Amos Saxby's head. It clicked its way along through the seconds, a light, echoing, persistent sound, the only sound in a tense, hushed atmosphere as Eric saw signs of real shock in Amos Saxby's eyes and Sam Saxby stood frozen near the window. In the silence Eric stared at Amos Saxby's tanned wrinkled features and for the first time saw hints of uncertainty behind the mask, signs of age and tiredness, and something else too. A savagery that was mounted in personal passions, the kind that left wounds and scars that might never heal.

'Frank Jennings's will?'

Eric nodded. 'The will by which Ellen Saxby came into possession of her second cousin's farm: Holton Hill Farm.'

Amos Saxby had recovered and his eyes glittered as he said, 'You have the floor, Mr Ward.'

Eric reached into his pocket and took out a folded sheet of paper. 'Perhaps you'll permit me to read the relevant clause to you, from the will itself.' When Amos Saxby gestured irritably, he went on. 'The clause reads as follows: *And to my cousin Ellen Saxby, of Eastgate Farm, Northumberland, in consideration of love and affection and knowing that she will carry out my wishes in the matter, I leave in fee simple the property known as Holton Hill, without encumbrances of any kind whatsoever* ... It was by virtue of that clause that, in 1969, Ellen Saxby came into possession of the farm.'

'That,' Amos Saxby said drily, 'is indisputable.'

'The important words for the purposes of Sandra Saxby,' Eric remarked, 'are these: *and knowing that she will carry out my wishes in the matter.*'

'And just why should they be so important to your client?' Amos Saxby demanded.

Eric took a deep breath. 'You'll have to forgive me boring you with the legal details, but it's necessary if I'm to explain what I'll be pointing out in court, if you refuse to reach a settlement with my client. That clause in the will of Frank Jennings raises an interesting legal point. It concerns the establishment of a trust.'

Amos Saxby stared gauntly at Eric. 'As far as I recall, no trusts were established by that damned will.'

'That's the point,' Eric replied calmly. 'Not on the face of it.'

'Explain,' Amos Saxby demanded, and his mouth was set in a grim line.

'I'll try,' Eric said. 'The general rule of law is that to create a trust nothing must be left to chance, or to ... interpretation. In other words the property must be identified, the person benefiting must be nominated, and the words used must clearly show an intention to create a trust.'

'As I said,' Amos Saxby interrupted. 'No trusts were mentioned in the Jennings' will.'

'Let me finish. While normally the law demands a strict form of words the courts will apply equitable principles, looking to the *intention* rather than the form. It means that even if a testator gives property by his will to a legatee, absolutely, that legatee *can* be subject to a trust for someone else's benefit, if he has been told during the lifetime of the testator that he was to take the property only subject to a trust. He must have agreed to such a trust, of course, either expressly or by implication — by his silence, for instance. In such cases, the courts will hold that a secret trust has been established.'

Amos Saxby was breathing heavily. 'I don't see what this has to do with the damned will.'

'A fully secret trust, Mr Saxby, arises where the will discloses neither the existence of the trust, nor its terms, but there is some indication from the evidence that such a trust exists.'

'Evidence? What evidence?'

Patiently Eric explained. 'There is a statement in Frank Jennings's will that gives the game away. He left Holton Hill Farm, on the face of it, to your wife Ellen absolutely, for her own benefit. But he used the words *knowing that she will carry out my wishes.*'

'So?'

'I will argue in court that these words constitute and point to the existence of a secret trust.'

'You're crazy!' Amos Saxby exploded. 'A trust for whose benefit?'

Calmly Eric Ward said, 'Let's look at the facts. The will is there. The words suggest a secret trust. Ellen Saxby takes the property and holds it for almost twenty years. She then creates an option to purchase, at a minimal sum, in favour of her son Jack Saxby. I will contend that Jack Saxby was the beneficiary of that secret trust—'

'I can't believe I'm listening to this!'

'I will contend that Ellen Saxby, under the terms of her second cousin's will, was never entitled beneficially to Holton Hill Farm, that she held it subject to a secret trust in favour of her youngest son, and that it was in completion of that trust that she created the option to purchase. I will further contend that where a trustee holds property in trust for another person, the trustee can in no circumstances either take a benefit from the trust nor hand over the benefit to some person other than the beneficiary. In other words, Mr Saxby, whether or not you succeed in fighting Sandra Saxby over the matter of conspiracy or fraud, you'll have to face this charge. That you inveigled your wife into betraying a trust, into an attempt to circumvent an agreement reached between Frank Jennings and your wife, and conspiracy or not, fraud or not, I'll nail you for breach of trust. And Sandra Saxby will win.'

'Dad—' It was Sam Saxby again; his voice was agonised.

'Alternatively, Mr Saxby,' Eric added mildly, 'you could reach the settlement out of court that I suggested a little while ago.'

Amos Saxby was staring at him as though he could hardly believe his ears. There should have been shock in his face; there should have been dismay. With a sinking feeling Eric Ward suddenly realized neither emotion was apparent. Amos Saxby was staring at him in amused disbelief. And the next moment the old man threw back his head and laughed. It was a great booming sound, a loud, shout of laughter.

'Lawyers!' he roared. 'My God, lawyers!' And he laughed again, a contemptuous roaring sound and the prickling at the back of Eric Ward's eyes became sharper as Amos Saxby laughed at him in an almost crazed disbelief.

* * *

It was as though they were suspended, riveted into a moment in time that was endless. The laughter reverberated from the walls of the room; Sam Saxby stood in frozen distress beside the window, and Eric Ward felt the tensions of the situation scratch at the nerve ends behind his eyes. The old man was standing with his hands on his hips, his legs braced apart, head back, laughing almost maniacally. The bellowing sound filled the room but there was little of genuine pleasure in it: a gasping pain lay at its core; deep down within the sound there was an animal snarling at the agony of its wounds, and overlying it all was the vicious contempt the old man had for the man who had tried to bait him. The ice-blue eyes were filmed with tears of laughter, and for the first time, staged though the laughter could have been, Eric guessed that Amos Saxby's theatricality had in fact deserted him. He was gripped by paroxysms of mingled anger, pain, and a deep-felt hurt; they found their expression in this great roaring sound, but in that expression lay Amos Saxby's own exposed vulnerability. Eric Ward knew that he had touched a nerve, and that he would now, perhaps, learn things that were not his to know.

'Lawyers,' Amos Saxby was gasping. 'You make me sick, all of you! The form ... the structure of things ... it's all that concerns you. You live in a bloody vacuum, you know that? You pride yourselves on being social scientists, of a sort; you deal with people, with their weaknesses and their crimes. You help and hinder them, teach and advise them. But you never *learn* yourselves! You never distinguish the realities; you never appreciate the truth, even when it stares you in the face!'

'Father ...' Sam Saxby's formality, his patent anxiety made him interrupt, but he still did not step forward. Amos Saxby ignored him. He glared at Eric Ward with a fierce, hating expression. He raised a hand; it was shaking slightly, fingers jabbing in Eric's direction and then convulsing, tensing, turning into a fist that thrust its menace in a defiant, uncompromising gesture.

'You can go to hell! You can spout about your schemes, your settlements, your secret trusts until you and that bitch are blue in the face! The fact is, young man, I'll see her in

143

the same hell as her husband before I give in. And as for this twaddle you talk—'

'Mr Saxby.' The pain was beginning to sharpen behind Eric's eyes and there were panics of his own beginning to rise in his chest. 'I see little point in continuing this conversation, but I must warn you—'

'Warn me, hell! This is my house, and I'll take no warnings in it!' The old man's face darkened, the skin mottling with anger, dark bruises appearing under his eyes as he glared viciously at Eric. There was almost a hint of madness in his voice as he suddenly shouted, 'You still don't seem to understand! Secret trusts ... you've got it all wrong! And it's time you got it straight, heard the way it was!'

Sam Saxby stirred now, uncoiling from his rigidity, almost stumbling forward to check his father. Amos Saxby brushed him aside impatiently, thrust away the restraining hand. He shook his fist at Eric Ward. 'You were right in one thing, my lawyer friend, but one thing only! Something did happen to *strain* relationships between me and Jack. Before that, it was all right. No essential problem, even if I didn't think he was the farmer *he* thought he was. But that was no great difference ...' He shot a vicious glance towards Sam Saxby. 'I was always bedevilled by the fact that I had three sons, not one of whom really had the capacity to run my farms as they should be run. It was why I determined to split the whole thing, give them a farm each. I talked it over with Ellen, and she was in agreement. My two farms to the older boys; hers, to Jack.'

Sam Saxby was retreating again, stepping back into the subservience he always seemed to show in the old man's presence.

Amos Saxby hardly saw him, and though he was staring at Eric Ward, he could hardly have been seeing him for a cloud of painful memory was etching images across his vision, turning his gaze inwards, backwards, seeking out the long-dead past and burning at the memory of it. 'And that was a nice, neat solution to it. Ellen and me, decent retirement.

144

Colin ... well, I always guessed maybe he'd sell up. He calls it adventurous; me, I call it foolhardy. But he always was weak, impressionable. Sam, here — a good enough farmer, but greedy, unable to accept that you have to *work* to build up a farm and a business; there are no short cuts to success, no easy way to create a farming empire, other, perhaps, than by inheritance. And Jack ... I had no objection to his taking Holton Hill Farm. It was Ellen's ... it was her decision. I saw no reason to oppose it, or suspect it. It provided for the youngest child. *Youngest child!*' Amos Saxby's eyes suddenly cleared and shot a malevolent glance towards Sam. 'But things changed when Sam came to see me, one day, here at the Vicarage.'

Sam Saxby could not meet the old man's glance. He looked towards Eric Ward nervously; there was an unspoken appeal in his eyes. But Amos Saxby could not be stopped now; he was launched on a flood of bitterness and memory, and he was out to draw blood.

'You see, Mr Ward, you've got to appreciate something about my eldest son Sam. He has something of me in him; something of the commitment, something of the drive, something of the *hunger* I had as a young man. But, even if I say so myself, he has something I did not: impatience. He knows what he wants but he can't wait to work for it. He wants it *now* — *whoever* it belongs to. He's greedy, you see; greedy for my land and possessions. And the more I have, he calculates, the more he'll get. As my favourite son, the only farmer. except for Jack, of course. And that's why he came to see me.'

'Dad, I don't think—'

The words died away under Amos Saxby's fierce glance. The old man smiled bitterly. 'It seems Sam had burned his fingers over a land deal in the Berwick area and was feeling upset; panicky even, at the thought that he was becoming financially unsound. It accounted for his attitude towards the wayleave over Eastgate Farm; it wasn't a serious matter and it blew over in the end; he wasted his money employing that barrister. But no matter; in an indirect way, it made his fortune — or so he hopes. Because this barrister, Francis, was working at your firm then, Ward, isn't that so? And he brought certain files with him, to Eastgate Farm. Sam here, he had the chance to look through those files. And then he brought them to me.'

Silence fell in the room. Amos Saxby's anger had now subsided, but the edge of bitterness remained in his voice. Eric Ward could not be certain whether the bitterness was directed towards his situation, or his son Sam.

'My eldest boy knew his duty, you see,' Amos Saxby was saying. 'He thought it only right that an old man should learn the truth. So he showed the files to me. What they disclosed ... well, very little, on the face of it. The possibility of a secret trust, certainly. To that extent, maybe you're right, Mr Ward. The possibility had occurred, you see, to the executors handling the Jennings estate. Their legal department had seen what you saw, and there was a brief correspondence. There was also a letter, from my wife. It was a strange letter; with hindsight, I can only suppose that it had been written at a time when she was under some strain.' His mouth twisted in an ugly, unpleasant fashion. 'The strain of loss, I would imagine. The letter puzzled me. I took it to her; asked her about it. She was scared; scared as hell.'

His glance dwelled on Eric Ward, thoughtfully. 'Funny thing. You live with someone half a lifetime, you think you know that person. You don't. It's just the exterior; inside the head — and the heart, it's all dark. Maybe even to the person himself — or herself. Sure, Ellen was like that. Confused, Scared. It was all so long ago, she said. As if that could possibly have made any difference.'

Once again, silence gathered around them. Amos Saxby was waiting, mockingly; there was still the twist of pain on his face, but he was waiting, playing a game, waiting for Eric to ask. And he had to ask.

'What ... what was the problem?'

Amos Saxby grinned, baring his teeth in a humourless grimace. 'Problem? That's one way of describing it. A simple enough problem, for all that. The problem was that after Ellen and I had been married a number of years, after she had borne me two sons, then, while I was working my guts out building up the farms she went and had an affair with a man twenty years older than her, her second cousin, no less, and was even stupid enough to have a child by him. And then, compounding the whole thing, she persuaded me the child was mine!'

Eric Ward's mouth was dry. 'Frank ... Frank Jennings was Jack's father?'

'You got it in one,' Amos Saxby said. 'Ellen was always fond of the old bastard and isn't there a saying that affection dwells in danger? The danger was a closer relationship ... The letter wasn't explicit, of course. She was merely answering some questions put to her by the Jennings's solicitors. But there were hints enough — raising questions which I asked. And she told me. It was so long ago, she said. For God's sake, as if time can wipe out something like that!'

'And that's when the decision was taken to try to override the option to purchase?'

'I wasn't having Holton Hill Farm going to the child masquerading as my son! For more than thirty years I hadn't know the truth; I'd been deceived. Frank Jennings seduced my wife and tried to give his farm to his bastard son! I wasn't going to have him laughing at me from his grave. He'd cuckolded me; his son wouldn't reap the benefit in land. *I'd* have the last laugh. It would become *my* land, to do with as I wished — and I intended — *intend* — giving it to *my* son.' He grinned again, wolfishly, and looked at Sam Saxby. 'My upright, caring, farming son — Samuel. The one who is the seeker after truth.'

Eric Ward hesitated. The pain behind his eyes was becoming worse now, and he was losing concentration. Stumblingly, he said, 'You ... you used the word *bastard* of Jack Saxby. It won't wash. He was born in wedlock.'

'But not *my* son.'

'You wouldn't be able to prove it. The court would not allow evidence tending to bastardize the issue. They simply would not allow—'

'Don't you understand?' Amos Saxby almost shouted. 'I don't give a damn what they'll allow! There'll be no settlement and I'll never give up Holton Hill Farm to the bitch who married Jack — the son of my wife's whoring with Frank Jennings!'

'And that's another thing,' Eric said desperately. 'Your wife. You said she was scared—'

'Scared as hell.' Amos Saxby paused, his eyes glittering. 'Oh yes, let's be clear about it. I'm sure she lived in her own private hell for thirty years and more — though things will have calmed down, no doubt, in the years that followed the death of Frank Jennings. But even so, there was always the chance. And she'd forgotten the letter ... probably didn't even know it was on the file from 1969. But she knew how I'd react if I ever found out. Exactly as I did.'

'You terrorized her—'

'I scared the living daylights out of her! I ranted and raved and made her life impossible for days! Until she did what I wanted. She conveyed Holton Hill Farm to me. And you can make what you want of it.'

'Duress—'

'To hell. Prove it. And let it all spill out in court. Do you think I care?' Amos Saxby leaned back, one elbow on the mantelpiece. He shook his head. 'I'm too old to care. I'll deny this conversation, and there'll be no proof. Crawl back to your client, Mr Ward, and advise her. Tell her to give it up. I'll never compromise; and a court action will cost her. And she'll lose.'

The pain was eddying in Eric Ward's skull, successive waves lancing into his nerve ends. He held on, grimly. 'I'm not so sure. You took advice from Paul Francis—'

'He seemed a good man to go to,' Amos Saxby said. 'I wanted to know how I could get around the option he drew up. And he told me to check its registration. From there, it was plain sailing.'

A wave of pain struck fiercely at Eric Ward's eyes. He fought the need to put his hand up to his head. 'Mrs Sandra Saxby is as determined as you. She'll not—'

'Mr Ward. I see no point in further discussion. I believe I hear a car in the drive. I am expecting visitors, to discuss a business proposition. Your presence is not required. This is my house. We have nothing further to say. It's time for you to take your leave.'

'Mr Saxby—'

'*Goodbye,* Mr Ward.'

There was nothing more Eric could do or say. Sam Saxby was walking towards him and his eyesight was blurring, the lance points scratching behind his eyes, the shuddering only minutes away unless he obtained relief. Sam Saxby was touching his arm, staring at him in a peculiar manner, aware perhaps of the physical distress Eric was in. Then the two of them were walking towards the door, and behind him, Amos Saxby snorted contemptuously.

They came out into the hallway and Amos Saxby called out in an imperious tone. 'Sam — the *back* door. Our visitors are arriving: Sandra Saxby's minion can use the tradesman's entrance.'

Sam Saxby murmured, in a tone lacking conviction, 'I'm sorry, Mr Ward,' and Eric allowed himself to be led to the left, along the corridor and away from the entrance hallway. A wave of nausea gripped him, swept over him and left him shaking.

'Are you all right?' Sam Saxby asked, his tone sharpening nervously.

Eric took a deep breath, fought against the nausea. He put his hand in his pocket, touched the phial of pilocarpine. 'Is ... is there a cloakroom I can use, for a moment?'

Sam Saxby hesitated, glanced back down the corridor. Then he walked towards the back doorway, stopped at another door on the left. 'There's a cloakroom here. You can use it. Afterwards, the back door leads out into the orchard. Follow the path around the side of the house and you'll come to the driveway where you've left your car. I'd better get back.'

Thankfully, Eric opened the door and went inside the barely furnished cloakroom. He fumbled in his pocket, brought out the phial and with shaking hands unstoppered it. He could hardly see himself in the mirror as the pain slashed across his eyes.

* * *

One of the side effects of taking the drug to relieve the agony behind his eyes was that when the pain receded, and the shaking stopped, he was left with a heightened sense of perception. He was not certain whether the pilocarpine normally had this effect; all he was aware of was that in the minutes that followed there would be a sharpening of the senses of smell and feel and hearing. It was possible that it was unreal — merely the increased confidence that alcohol could also bring, but as he stared at himself in the mirror he felt the usual lightness of head, the clarity of mental vision and the sharpness of hearing what he now associated with the relief from pain.

He glanced at his watch. A couple of minutes had passed; he was not fully recovered, but in a little while he would be fit to drive. It was time he left the cloakroom of Amos Saxby's Old Vicarage, made his way out through the humiliation of the back door, and then he would sit in his car until he had fully recovered.

It would give him time to consider what he had learned, digest the story Amos Saxby had told him, consider the implication of it all, and then decide how he was to advise Sandra Saxby. One thing was certain: Amos Saxby had browbeaten his wife into conveying the farm to him. Duress or not, the conveyance had then been made with the express intention of defeating the option to purchase.

It left Sandra Saxby with a surfeit of choice: duress and an avoidable contract; the secret trust, even more believable now Eric knew that Frank Jennings had been providing for the mother of his son; and a clear conspiracy between Amos and Ellen Saxby, with Sam edging even more into the picture.

It left only Colin Saxby out. Eric wondered idly where he fitted into it all. It had been Sam who told Amos about the file, but the resultant row with Ellen, known to Sam, may or may not have been known to Colin. And yet ... Eric considered the matter. Why had Jack Saxby gone charging out to the Old Vicarage to confront his father? It *could* have been the result of Eric's advice about the defeat of the option ... but the action had seemed somewhat impetuous, when he had already, in effect, asked Eric to begin legal proceedings. What if Jack had been told about his birthright? And if he *had* known, who would have told him?

Not Sam Saxby, Eric mused, certainly not Amos Saxby's greedy heir-at-law. And Colin Saxby? *He* had denied knowing the cause of the trouble, though that could have been a defensiveness towards outsiders. On the other hand, he had certainly known that the decision to try defeating the option had been Amos's doing, not Ellen Saxby's.

Not that it made much difference either way. His advice to Sandra Saxby now would have to be that her only chance of justice for her dead husband would be to go through with the action against Amos, the father-in-law she hated. A settlement was out of the question: Eric knew that now, for he recognized the poison that lay in the old man's veins. Amos Saxby was an unforgiving man, and he visited the old sins upon the son until he died, and now, upon Sandra Saxby.

Quietly Eric let himself out of the cloakroom and closed the door behind him. The hallway was empty and he was tempted, for a moment, to make his way out through the front door of the Old Vicarage after all. Then, hearing the voices in the room where he had left Amos Saxby, he decided to make as dignified an exit from the old man's house as possible. Time for confrontations when they met in court.

The door was latched, an old-fashioned piece of iron that he was forced to lift, the kind of latch that had been common enough when he was a boy but out of place, he felt, in the Old Vicarage. And yet not out of place. The house was old, rambling — unlike Amos Saxby. He could hear his voice now, booming out of the room Eric had left.

He lifted the latch, began to open the door.

'Enough of the pleasantries,' he heard Amos Saxby say in his loud, arrogant voice. 'Let's get down to business.'

Eric stepped out, paused in face of the drizzling rain. 'You've been trying to persuade me to put my money in Stoneleigh Enterprises all this time, Colin, but without success. So what's new this time, to make me change my mind?'

The words washed over Eric Ward, their import vague and yet ringing with a clarity his heightened senses seized on, clung to avidly. He stood in the doorway, he listened for a few minutes, and then as the questions mounted in his mind he stepped back into the house and closed the door softly behind him.

The latch dropped into place with a sharp, echoing click.

* * *

There was something stagey about it, a *tableau vivant*, a set scene from a West End production. Enter the corpse. If Amos Saxby had staged it there would perhaps have been more noise and thunder. Instead there was complete, surprised silence as they all stared at him standing in the doorway, the unconsidered, unbidden guest. Amos Saxby had moved away from the fireplace and now sat sprawled in one of the deep armchairs, his long legs splayed out in front of him. Sam Saxby stood behind the chair, one hand on its back and facing the two were Colin Saxby and the Honourable Antony Stoneleigh.

The silence was expectant. Amos Saxby's forehead was furrowed with hints of anger: he did not enjoy surprises. Sam

Saxby was shaken, as though fearful of his father's wrath in not actually having seen the interloper off the premises. But if Colin Saxby expressed puzzlement in his features, Antony Stoneleigh was clearly indifferent to Eric Ward's appearance in the doorway. He had been about to speak; now he glanced towards Amos Saxby as though expecting him to give a lead. Amos Saxby did so, in appropriate fashion.

'What the bloody hell are you doing here?'

'Mr Saxby—'

'I thought you'd gone! Sam, didn't you see him off the premises?'

Sam Saxby tried to say something but the words died in his throat. He shot a swift glance in Colin Saxby's direction and something in that glance induced nervousness in the younger brother. The feeling was quickly communicated to the old man, and his suspicious eyes narrowed, flicking quick glances between Eric Ward and Colin Saxby.

'I wasn't eavesdropping,' Eric Ward explained. 'Not deliberately, at least. I had an attack ...'

'What do you want, Ward?' Amos Saxby interrupted. 'I've heard you out; there's nothing more to say between us, not as far as I'm concerned.'

Eric hesitated. 'It's what you said a moment ago. I was just leaving ... I caught what you said.'

Amos Saxby scowled. 'And what was so important about what I said?'

'I ... I'm not sure. But it surprised me. You said they've been trying to persuade you to put money into Stoneleigh Enterprises.'

Eric Ward was staring at Amos Saxby; there was a movement across to his left, and he could not be sure whether it was Colin Saxby or Stoneleigh. Amos Saxby's cold eyes glittered. 'You were surprised ... why should it surprise you? An investment of this kind—'

'I was surprised,' Eric Ward blurted out, 'because I understood you had *already* invested in the Stoneleigh Enterprises project.'

The silence lengthened, sharpening about them as Amos Saxby glared at Eric Ward. He raised a hand, rubbed it thoughtfully against his mouth. When he spoke his tone was gentler, but it was the softness of a predatory animal lulling its prey into carelessness. 'Why should you believe I had *already* invested in Stoneleigh Enterprises, Mr Ward?'

Eric held his glance. 'I've been making enquiries. Their object was to discover ... facts that you've now divulged to me anyway. But in employing an enquiry agent to find out why you and Jack Saxby were estranged, other information came to light.'

'Other information?'

'My informant told me that you are reputed to have a significant shareholding in Stoneleigh Enterprises.'

'Dad—' Colin Saxby's intervention was cut short by a peremptory wave of his father's hand.

'Tell me more, Mr Ward.'

Eric Ward hesitated. There was a tension in the air he could not yet understand, any more than he could fully understand the excitement in his own veins. His thoughts were confused, as he remembered snatches of conversation, snippets of information which seemed to be unrelated, and yet in their very illogicality seemed to be bringing about some kind of linking pattern in his mind. He shook his head, trying to clear the jumble of information, aware of the drug-induced sharpness behind his eyes. 'At the party given for Sir John Freshfield I was told by Freshfield's somewhat indiscreet financial adviser that Stoneleigh Enterprises were unlikely to get the support they were seeking from Sir John's bank. And then, more recently, I heard that you had a substantial shareholding in the company. Yet today I heard you say you had no such holding. It doesn't make sense.'

'Neither to you,' Amos Saxby said softly, 'nor to me.' He turned to Colin Saxby. 'What about you?'

Colin Saxby was pale. He flicked an uneasy glance towards Sam Saxby and then shook his head. 'I don't know what this is all about. This story ...'

His words died away, uncertainly. Amos Saxby turned again to Eric Ward in the heavy silence that followed. 'Your informant?'

'Is reliable.'

'Yet I do not have any shares in the company.' Amos Saxby smiled suddenly, a winning, charming, theatrical smile directed towards Antony Stoneleigh. 'Which does not mean someone might not have *said* I had a holding in the company. Though for what reason, I cannot imagine.'

Something moved at the back of Eric Ward's mind, something unpleasant, tinged with horror. 'The reason ... it might have been to boost confidence in the company. Colin is already in deeply; a significant shareholding by you, it would have looked good in a presentation to Freshfield's and others.'

Amos Saxby's smile broadened. 'Interesting ... Yes, I see that. The fact is, Mr Ward, Colin has been pressing me for some time to take up a very large holding. I've resisted.' He paused, eyeing Eric sardonically. 'You're becoming something of a catalyst in this family circle, Mr Ward. It amuses me. A little piece of information like that ... I'll give you another piece now, and see what you make of that. Maybe you can even cap it ... for none of us individually sees a whole picture, do we? Colin came to see me some time ago. He pressed me to take up the shares, told me it would be a fine investment. I told him to go to hell, in my usual polite manner — if he chose to sell good farming land and risk the proceeds in wild schemes that was his affair. But, at the time, I was under some pressure ...' His blue eyes clouded momentarily, and Eric wondered for a brief moment how much the old man had been really shaken by the death of his wife. 'Anyway, I was concerned about the pending litigation and I told Colin that if he got Jack off my back, made him drop the threatened suit, I'd invest in Stoneleigh Enterprises. It was a weak moment on my part, you understand, but I would have stuck to it. The fact is, of course, I was never called upon to do it, because in the event Colin never did persuade Jack.'

'Instead, he told him the facts surrounding his birth,' Eric said.

Amos Saxby straightened in his chair. The veins in the back of his hands stood out like cords suddenly as he gripped the chair arms. He stared at Colin Saxby. 'Is that so? I'd wondered about that. I thought maybe Sam — malicious and greedy — had arranged it to make relationships even worse between us. That was unjust of me. So it was Colin, hey? I wonder why he did that?'

They were speaking of Colin Saxby as though he were not there. The man stood stiffly, staring at his father, and his lips were grimly set, his face pale. Behind him, the Honourable Antony Stoneleigh moved uneasily, brushing his fair hair from his eyes in a nervous gesture as the old man watched sardonically, playfully, a cat watching the terrified mice.

'It might have been desperation,' Eric Ward said quietly.

Amos Saxby continued to stare at his son. Sam Saxby shuffled, and seemed about to speak but then subsided again, falling back into a role Eric now clearly saw him fitting: the intriguer behind the scenes, never really coming out into the open, but seeking intelligently for his main chance.

'Desperation,' Amos Saxby repeated, rolling the word around his tongue as though he enjoyed it. 'Why should he be desperate?'

'I don't know,' Eric replied thoughtfully. 'But from what's been said, I could hazard a guess. Your son invested heavily in Stoneleigh Enterprises. He also wanted *your* financial support. He must have pressed the case strongly, if it came down to a bargaining situation with you. And that must mean Colin had pressing reasons to want your support. So, when he took your line, went to Jack and asked him to drop the suit against you and your wife, how would he react to a refusal? With anger, maybe; with passion? A worried man can be an indiscreet one. Maybe when Jack refused point blank to back down Colin played his wild card. Maybe he told Jack that he could never win against Amos Saxby

156

because of the reason Amos Saxby had for the disinheritance. And that would be why Jack then came charging up here; too angry and ashamed even to tell his wife, but confronting you and his mother in the Old Vicarage—'

'And bringing about his mother's death, eventually,' the old man said bitterly. 'People compound their sins ... But where, I wonder, would Colin have discovered the secret, known only to ...'

His voice whispered into silence and Eric Ward looked at Sam Saxby, standing protectively behind his father's chair. From the momentary panic in Sam Saxby's eyes Eric knew where the information had come from. 'Quite a family you have, Mr Saxby,' he said drily.

The smile still hovered around the old man's mouth, but it had a cynical twist. 'Perhaps the family I deserve,' he said bitterly. 'However, where is all this leading us, Mr Ward? A brother who seeks to sow dissension amongst his rivals; a second brother who blurts out a family secret; a third brother who kills his mother by raging at her and me in this room. Where does it all lead to, except unpleasantness? And the further question, as to why Colin is so keen to have me, then and now, invest in Stoneleigh Enterprises?'

Antony Stoneleigh stepped forward before Eric could reply. He seemed at ease, and confident, his grey eyes holding a slight hint of amusement, his manner a relaxed disavowal of having any involvement with these petty family affairs. In moving forward he took the centre of the stage that Amos Saxby always seemed to erect about himself, and he held it with a confidence in his own capability. 'I think,' he said, 'I had better say something in all this.'

Colin Saxby started forward, laid a hand on Stoneleigh's arm. 'Wait a minute, Antony, I don't think—'

'You never did, Colin, not with clarity,' Stoneleigh interrupted brutally. 'That's been the problem.'

'But there's still the chance—'

'No chance,' Stoneleigh said swiftly. 'It's all too late, dear boy. Freshfield's have turned us down, and the whispers are going about. It's time you faced facts.' He turned to look at Amos Saxby. 'And the one fact is, Colin's in trouble.'

Amos Saxby's cold blue eyes narrowed. 'Explain.'

Stoneleigh waved a negligent hand. 'Easily told. The project is a sound one; ahead of its time; it can make us all rich. But bankers are blinkered men. I'll say that about Colin — he wasn't blinkered. He saw the possibilities and put everything he had into the project. But we needed a stronger financial base if we were to persuade Freshfield's. I found other backers, but was still some sixty thousand short. Without it, we could be straight down the drain. That's when Colin came up trumps.'

'And how exactly did he do that?'

'He gave Stoneleigh Enterprises a financial guarantee for that amount.'

'He doesn't have the money,' Sam Saxby blurted out in surprise.

'But *I* do,' Amos Saxby said after a short silence, and there was a tired edge to his voice suddenly.

'That's right,' Antony Stoneleigh said. 'And the guarantee was *signed in your name.*'

The room fell silent. Eric Ward, still standing in the doorway shifted slightly, uneasy as other thoughts began to crowd into his brain, other possibilities surging to the surface. He watched Amos Saxby's face, noting its greyness, the deep lines etched around the mouth becoming more marked as the weaknesses of his family were exposed about him.

'I signed no such guarantee,' Amos Saxby announced at last, heavily.

'So I understand,' Stoneleigh replied. *'Now.'* He paused, as theatrical as Amos. 'The thing is, what do we do about it at this point of time? The possible alternatives are not numerous, after all. Freshfield's have turned us down, but with your sixty thousand we could still pull through, get American backing and make the venture pay. But if you don't support us with this investment — which I assure you will bring in a good return — what happens to Colin? If that guarantee — which, clearly, he forged — is shown to be worthless there are a number of people who will claim to have entered the investment on the strength of a forged prospectus — *Colin's* forgery, because I took the guarantee in good faith. He was shall we say, over-enthusiastic, when he thought he saw his investment slipping away. The question now is, will you retrieve the situation?' He paused again, waiting, and then in the silence turned to Colin Saxby. 'I'm sorry, old man, but there really was no alternative. It's time it was out in the open. Your father wasn't going to invest any other way.'

'And you think I'll invest to save my son from jail?' Amos sneered.

Stoneleigh grinned unpleasantly. 'You've lost one son, Mr Saxby. I don't think you're wanting to lose another.'

* * *

And yet there was still something wrong, something unsaid, an unspecific statement that hung in the air about them. Eric Ward felt it like a prickling upon his skin, a menace that was almost tangible. There was something missing in the tangle of family relationships, a fact that was still loose, not pinned down, a facet of a man's character, the expectations of a gambler who needed to be certain, and ruthless and precise. It was there in this room, in this house, in this family.

'I wonder what else Colin might have told Jack, when he tried to persuade him to give up the suit? Then, or later?'

Eric's words caused a strange reaction.

Colin Saxby jerked visibly as though he had been stung; Sam and his father seemed puzzled, unsure as to what he was getting at, but in Antony Stoneleigh's studied carelessness there was yet a hint of tension.

'What else was there to tell him?' Amos Saxby growled, 'What else we haven't heard?'

'Nothing, perhaps,' Eric replied. 'Except ... *did Colin tell Jack about the guarantee?*' In the silence Amos Saxby turned his head and stared at his second son. Colin Saxby's defences were openly crumbling; his assertiveness and self-confidence had gone with Stoneleigh's revelations and now this last question seemed to be sowing seeds of destruction in him, and he almost wilted, sagging about the shoulders while his face displayed a sudden panic.

'Well?' Amos Saxby demanded truculently.

It was Antony Stoneleigh who spoke. 'There would have been no point, no sense in confiding to Jack Saxby that he had forged a guarantee. Colin would have gained nothing from it—'

'Except sympathy,' Eric Ward argued, 'and perhaps the gain of another lever to get Jack to drop the suit against Amos. It would have been logical, in fact: once Jack refused to stay his hand for Amos's or Ellen's sake, he might have been persuaded to do so for *Colin's* sake, to save him from the exposure to a criminal charge.'

'Rubbish,' Stoneleigh said explosively. 'Colin?'

Colin Saxby shuddered slightly at his father's tone but he did not look at him; instead, his eyes were fixed on Antony Stoneleigh and once again Eric Ward felt the prickling of his skin as he saw the doubts and the fears and the hidden suspicions crawling in Colin Saxby's eyes.

'One moment,' Eric Ward interrupted, in a peremptory tone. 'Mr Saxby, *did* Jack make no mention to you of the forged guarantee?'

Amos Saxby shook his head.

'Well, if Jack did know about the guarantee,' Eric went on, 'if he *had* been told about it, I wonder what his reaction might have been? He had things on his mind at the time — the circumstances surrounding his birth, the deliberate attempt to defeat the option — and that's why he stormed out here to the Vicarage. But if he learned later about the guarantee . . .'

'There was nothing he could do,' Antony Stoneleigh said quietly. 'Once it became public knowledge, Colin would be ruined, as he still can be.' The hint of menace, of pressure upon Amos Saxby hung in the air, but Eric Ward's thoughts were already elsewhere, his mind tumbling pieces of information, mingled with questions, over and over. He turned to Colin Saxby. '*Did* you tell Jack about the guarantee?'

There was a short silence. Colin Saxby's face was grey, his eyes evasive. He seemed unwilling to meet Eric's glance, but there was also an odd tension in his attitude towards Antony Stoneleigh. 'I ... I did tell him. It was like a last chance. I went to see him, that morning ...'

'When?'

Colin Saxby licked his lips. 'The ... the day he died.' His voice was suddenly shaky, a nervous pleading had crept into it as though he was begging to be asked no more, anxious that no further digging should be done, for his own peace of mind. But the flash of suspicious horror that had crossed Eric Ward's mind earlier was now beginning to take form, seeping to the front of his mind, hardening into the reality of possibility. Jack Saxby had not been Amos's son; he had been the offspring of Frank Jennings, lacking the Saxby self-centred ruthlessness. But he had been surrounded by them until, thrust away as an outsider, could he not have looked about him, seen clearly the kind of people his half-brothers and old Amos were — and decided to be like them?

'The night of the Freshfield party,' Eric said slowly. 'you came by car, with Sam?'

'He dropped me,' Sam Saxby said quickly, urgent to seek no involvement in the heightening tension of the room. 'Then went on to meet Mr Stoneleigh.'

Colin Saxby nodded, relieved at the change of topic. 'That's right, I went to Antony's for a few drinks, after I'd parked outside Grey's.'

Eric stared at him. 'The flat is nearby?'

'Just around the corner.'

'And after the party?'

'You know,' Colin Saxby said peevishly. 'You were there. We went to the club. And got drunk.'

'Drunker,' Stoneleigh said contemptuously, and then swung back to Amos Saxby. 'But I don't know why we're talking about this. I'm here to persuade you to invest in Stoneleigh Enterprises. It's still a viable proposition if you do invest; if you don't, it goes to the wall and if you don't back Colin's guarantee he'll face criminal charges. The situation is quite simple and I'm disinclined to waste time listening to this question and answer—'

'Do you remember Hilda?' Ward asked Stoneleigh.

'Of course,' Stoneleigh replied snappishly.

'She was pretty drunk too, wasn't she?'

Stoneleigh stared at him, making no reply and Eric turned to Colin Saxby. 'She was drunk, wasn't she? Drunk enough, maybe, to go out like a light once she hit the bed. Mr Stoneleigh's bed.'

'My private life—' Stoneleigh began angrily, but Eric ignored him.

'Well, Colin? Was she pretty stoned?' Colin Saxby was unwilling to answer; the anxieties lurking behind his eyes were more nakedly exposed now and though he tried to thrust them away, regain control, he was unsuccessful. 'She ... I don't know ... I suppose she *was* pretty far gone.'

'You left the club about two,' Eric said. 'And couldn't find your keys.'

Colin Saxby's mouth was tortured. 'That ... that's right. I lost—'

'And Stoneleigh stayed behind, in a bedroom at the club. With Hilda.' He paused, then looked at Stoneleigh. 'And she was drunk. Almost insensible.'

'Now look here—'

But Colin Saxby interrupted Stoneleigh's angry gesture. 'What ... what are you trying to say?'

They were all waiting, listening, wondering, and the tension was almost palpable, a physical thing that affected their nerve ends, quickened their breathing, brought pressure upon their hearts and lungs. But Eric was not yet sure what he was leading towards ... the view was half-formed, and yet he suspected as he looked into Colin Saxby's panicked eyes that the images that crossed his mind were already buried deep, restrained and confined in Colin Saxby's terrified brain.

'You haven't been able to bring yourself to ask the questions,' Eric said slowly. 'That's it ... you couldn't ask, because of the consequences.'

Amos Saxby, out of the limelight, shuffled impatiently. 'Consequences? What consequences?'

'The exposure of the forged guarantee,' Eric said. 'And the part Colin played in the murder of Jack Saxby.'

Amos Saxby shook his head like a puzzled bull, then dragged himself out of his chair, rose shakily to his feet. He was no longer in command; the actors were beyond his control. 'What the hell are you driving at, Ward?'

'I don't have the proofs,' Eric Ward said quietly, 'but I can understand now how it happened.'

Colin Saxby made a soft, frightened sound in his throat but Amos Saxby was glowering fiercely in Eric Ward's direction. 'For God's sake, man, stop pussyfooting around! What the hell are you on about?'

Eric took a deep breath. 'Colin told Jack he wanted you to invest in Stoneleigh Enterprises, and that you *would,* if he could get Jack to back off the action he had started.'

'I knew he never would,' Amos Saxby said with bitter satisfaction.

'And you were right. Then, when Colin also told him why you were trying to defeat the option he came raging out here. None of that did Colin any good; self-centred, like all the Saxbys, he still wanted to get the support he needed for his own foolish investments with Stoneleigh. So he went to see Jack again — and begged him to stop the action, because otherwise he'd be charged with forgery. The truth would be bound to come out, eventually. But Jack's reaction was surprising. I think he decided to act like a Saxby himself.'

Amos furrowed his brow. 'What the hell do you mean by that?'

'The Saxbys,' Eric said cuttingly, 'are of a kind. Ruthless, self-centred, egotistical — they go for the jugular, irrespective of what it means to others, even their own family. You, old man, you set the tone. You browbeat your wife and helped her into her grave; Sam followed the same track, bringing to your attention the Saxby file and its incriminating evidence against your wife; Colin was prepared to tell Jack those things that would help him in his own situation. You were all three cast in the same mould. And Jack, who had *thought* himself to be a Saxby and then found he wasn't, decided to join you. He had none of your blood, Amos, but you'd tainted him.'

'I don't understand,' Amos Saxby glowered.

'When Colin told him about the guarantee, asking for his help, I think all the bitterness, the hurt, the *hate,* came bubbling to the surface. Jack *became* a Saxby: he decided to use the information not to help Colin, but to do anything he could to hurt the family.'

'There was nothing he could do,' Stoneleigh said swiftly, waving his hand in a deprecating gesture.

'Wrong. The exposure of the forged guarantee would involve one of Amos's precious *real* sons in scandal. Who could tell how far the ripples would spread, when Jack brought his own action? And Amos himself, he'd be hurt, for all that I think Jack wanted to strike out, hurt, damage the Saxbys who had rejected him. He wouldn't even have worked it all out logically.'

'My dear man,' Antony Stoneleigh drawled, pushing back an errant lock of fair hair in a studied gesture, 'all this supposition—'

'But he would, of course, be hurting someone else, too,' Eric said quietly.

Colin Saxby moved nervously. Antony Stoneleigh stood very still, watching Eric keenly. 'What exactly is that supposed to mean?'

'On the day Jack Saxby died,' Eric said, 'the Freshfield deal — the support of his merchant bank — it was still a real possibility, to you at least, if not to Freshfield's financial adviser. You couldn't afford to have Jack Saxby putting your big deal at risk. So what Colin told you, when he came to your flat—'

Colin Saxby stepped forward, scared; Stoneleigh put out a hand to stop him, but Eric carried on swiftly. 'You did tell him, didn't you, Colin? You explained that you had told Jack, but that Jack hadn't been sympathetic, that he had reacted in a manner you'd not expected. You told Stoneleigh you were afraid Jack would blow the whole guarantee thing sky-high just at the time Stoneleigh was hoping to net Freshfield! So what happened then, Colin? You had already been drinking ... maybe you were a bit fuddled. But what did Stoneleigh say? That he'd better see Jack, after the party at the club? That he had no car, but would borrow the one you had — Sam's — to go down later to the Quayside to see Jack, to remonstrate with him? You never *lost* your keys, Colin did you? You *gave* them to him!'

'Colin—' Stoneleigh warned.

'And later you had to cover up when, drunk, you found Sam, the car gone because Stoneleigh had left the club before *we* had, having dropped the insensible Hilda — and the first suspicions of what Stoneleigh might do had begun to crawl into your mind.'

'I swear I—'

'Or perhaps you always knew what he was going to do,' Eric said contemptuously.

They were all staring at the haunted face of Colin Saxby when Antony Stoneleigh broke the silence. 'As you said, Ward, you've no damned proof.'

But his voice was low and shaky.

* * *

Detective-Superintendent Jenkins expressed himself satisfied once again with the standard of the coffee served to him at Francis, Shaw and Elder; he also expressed considerable satisfaction at the progress in the investigations into the death of Jack Saxby. The lady he described as the 'blonde bombshell', Hilda, did indeed have only hazy recollections of the night in question and could furnish no alibi for Stoneleigh since she had fallen into a drunken stupor almost as soon as he had taken her to the back room. Similarly, there was forensic evidence to tie Stoneleigh to the car: his defence lawyer would, of course, argue that such traces proved nothing — they could be the result of an earlier occupancy. But the clinching evidence lay with Colin Saxby. His guilt-ridden suppression of the questions in his own mind was, he claimed, now over — 'and he's singing,' Freddie Jenkins said cheerfully, 'like a hoarse budgerigar. He's fluttering frantically to escape a clear involvement: he says he gave the keys to Stoneleigh but never *dreamt* Stoneleigh would use the car to kill Jack when Jack wouldn't be persuaded. Not that we believe it ... Colin Saxby was too quick with the lost keys story that very night to have had a clear conscience. But ... well, we can nail Stoneleigh with the story, and there's plenty enough on Colin Saxby to see him inside for a long stretch, Queen's Evidence or not.'

Yes, Detective-Superintendent Freddie Jenkins was well satisfied, with the way things had turned out in the Saxby affair; it looked as though it would all turn out neatly with Stoneleigh in custody, and Colin Saxby co-operative. All quite satisfactory.

* * *

Joseph Francis, senior partner in Francis, Shaw and Elder held quite a different view of the circumstances. He came into Eric's office after Jenkins had gone and stood for a little while, staring out over the city, his hands locked behind his back, fingers tightly clasped. When he spoke his voice was cold.

'You've seen the judgment in *Saxby?*'

'I have it here,' Eric replied.

166

'You handled it badly,' Joseph Francis said crisply. 'We ... the firm comes out of the case with a tarnished reputation. It was what I warned you about, right at the beginning, but you were always too damned independent. If you'd followed my advice, played down certain aspects, but no ... independent. Such independence must lead, in my view, to a parting of the ways. That woman Sandra Saxby — she says she'll be suing us. It's not good enough. It could have been averted.'

'I don't think so.'

'I do. If I'd handled it ... but it's of no consequence. I no longer feel, Eric, that Francis, Shaw and Elder have the necessary confidence in you to support a continued and satisfactory relationship. I think the partnership should now come to an end.' He had not met Eric's eyes when he said it and there had been no handshake when he left.

Yet the interview, and its result had not been entirely unexpected on Eric Ward's part. The two solicitors had not been at one throughout the case, and anyway, blood was thicker than partnership agreements. Joseph wanted to protect his son Paul: when Sandra Saxby brought her claim against the firm, for negligence, a solicitor — Eric Ward — would recently have left the firm. It would never actually be *said*, but the inference would be drawn by many that it was Eric's negligence that was being criticized, and had been the cause of his leaving Francis, Shaw and Elder. The career of Paul Francis at the Bar would remain unsullied.

It all served to illustrate, really, the gulf that could yawn between the concepts of law and justice. Paul would escape — even though he was guilty of a breach of professional ethics. Sandra Saxby and Amos Saxby would fight their increasingly bitter battles for ever — and the only scrap of justice that emerged from *that* situation was that in the end, when Sandra was delivered of her child, the wishes of Frank Jennings would to some degree have been respected in spite of all that had happened: Holton Hill Farm, or the proceeds of its sale, would go to a child of his blood.

But for Eric, there was little justice. And yet he hardly cared any more. He was tired and frightened by the prospect that faced him. He could dwell on old Amos Saxby still nursing the old enmities but now forced to do what he hated doing; on Sam Saxby waiting for his father to die; on the widowed, pregnant Sandra Saxby still viciously determined to get her pound of legal flesh as well as her financial fat. He was well out of that whole family affair.

And he had his own realities to face.

He could pick up the phone and call Anne Morcomb. He loved her — he had known that since his visits to her home two years ago, and he knew that she was in love with him; she had made it plain, in the flat in Montague Court. It would be so easy, to pick up the phone, say the words, and the problems could disappear — she had money, he would not need to face the possibility of blindness alone, nor the prospect of a damaged career. It was all so easy, only a phone call away. So easy, yet so impossible.

For there was still the gulf of years, still the essentially male pride that thrust him away from the thought of a financial dependence upon her, still the stubborn refusal to allow himself to turn his back on the deeply personal threat that lay in his future. If he phoned, she could find herself married to a helpless, blind, ageing man whose affliction could make him bitter. She was better without him — whatever she felt for him.

There was a phone call to make — but not to Anne. It was time now he faced up to the bleakness of his future and dwelled with his own danger. The ophthalmic surgeon lived in Gosforth; Eric's hands were cold as he dialled the number.

'Mr Callaghan? This is Eric Ward. I've reached my decision. I'll take the chance on the operation.'

Then he stayed on in the office as the darkening evening changed the shape and form of the room.

* * *

Extract from the judgment of Justice Semple, in *Saxby v National Bank Ltd and Another*.

'The option was an estate contract with Class C (iv), as to which section 13(2) of the Land Charges Act 1925 says it shall be void as against a purchaser of the land charged if it is not registered. The same section emphasizes, however, that this applies only in favour of a particular kind of purchaser — namely, a purchaser of the legal estate for money or money's worth. The key words are *for money or money's worth*. They mean an adequate sum. The amount paid by Amos Saxby for Holton Hill Farm was not adequate in this sense: to suggest so would be to condone fraud of the worst description.

But apart from this, it is my opinion that the provisions are not applicable in any case where fraud exists. It is true that in *Re Monolithic Building Co* a purchaser *was* protected even though he had full notice of the existence of the charge but *he* paid *full value*. I agree with Lord Denning, MR, when he says:

No court in this land will allow a person to keep an advantage which he has obtained by fraud. No judgment of a court ... can be allowed to stand if it has been obtained by fraud. Fraud unravels everything ...

The conveyance was executed to deprive Jack Saxby of the benefit of the option. That was a fraud on Jack Saxby. Amos Saxby was a party to that fraud: he cannot be allowed to take advantage of it to the prejudice of Jack Saxby's estate; nor can the executors of the estate of Ellen Saxby take advantage of it. The estate of Ellen Saxby will accordingly honour that option by transferring Holton Hill Farm to Mrs Jack Saxby, the conveyance to Amos Saxby being declared to be of no effect ... I am not required to make answer in respect of other issues raised: the effect of duress upon Ellen Saxby; the possible existence of a secret trust; the matter of conspiracy between Amos, Ellen and Samuel Saxby. The whole matter rests upon and is determined as a result of fraud against Jack Saxby.

It looks to me, nevertheless, as if there may be claims against some solicitors or others for negligence in some stages of this litigation. On this I cannot, of course, rule ...'

THE END

ROY LEWIS BOOKS

ERIC WARD MYSTERIES
BOOK 1: THE SEDLEIGH HALL MURDER
BOOK 2: THE FARMING MURDER

INSPECTOR JOHN CROW
Book 1: A LOVER TOO MANY
Book 2: ERROR OF JUDGMENT
Book 3: THE WOODS MURDER
Book 4: MURDER FOR MONEY
Book 5: MURDER IN THE MINE
Book 6: A COTSWOLDS MURDER
Book 7: A FOX HUNTING MURDER
Book 8: A DARTMOOR MURDER

More ROY LEWIS books coming soon!
Join our mailing list to be the first to hear about them
http://www.joffebooks.com/contact/

Made in the USA
Monee, IL
04 December 2022